RITE OF PASSAGE

RITE OF PASSAGE

BY
RICHARD WRIGHT

Afterword by Arnold Rampersad

HarperCollins*Publishers*

The publishers would like to thank Ellen Wright and Michel Fabre for permission to use the chronology that appeared in *Richard Wright Reader*, copyright © 1978 by Ellen Wright and Michel Fabre, HarperPerennial; and The Yale Collection of American Literature, Beinecke Rare Book and Manuscript Library, Yale University, for the use of manuscript material from their library.

Rite of Passage
Copyright © 1994 by Ellen Wright
Afterword copyright © 1994 by Arnold Rampersad
Title page illustration copyright © 1994 by David Diaz
For information address HarperCollins Children's Books, a division of HarperCollins Publishers, 10 East 53rd Street, New York, NY 10022.

Library of Congress Cataloging-in-Publication Data
Wright, Richard, 1908–1960.
Rite of passage / by Richard Wright ; afterword by Arnold Rampersad.
    p.   cm.
Includes bibliographical references.
Summary: When fifteen-year-old Johnny Gibbs is told that he is really a foster child, he runs off into the streets of Harlem and meets up with a gang that wants him to participate in a mugging. Includes criticism of Wright's fiction.
ISBN 0-06-023419-9. — ISBN 0-06-023420-2 (lib. bdg.)
1. Afro-American teenage boys—New York (N.Y.)—Fiction.   2. Gangs—New York (N.Y.)—Fiction.   3. Harlem (New York, N.Y.)—Fiction. [1. Runaways—Fiction.   2. Gangs—Fiction.   3. Afro-Americans—Fiction. 4. Harlem (New York, N.Y.)—Fiction.]   I. Title.
PS3545.R815R58   1994   93-2473
813'.52—dc20   CIP
                                                                        AC

Typography by Stefanie Rosenfeld
2   3   4   5   6   7   8   9   10
❖
First Edition

CONTENTS

Rite of Passage 1

Afterword by Arnold Rampersad.................................117

Selected Bibliography...145

Chronology..147

I

Johnny slouched down behind his desk, clutching his battered reading book, his mind winging away. The white woman teacher's silver voice caressed his ears droningly, lulling him into the depths of a daydream centered about a bowl of steaming beef stew waiting for him upon the kitchen table. Beneath the measured rhythm of the teacher's voice came the quiet ticking of the wall clock, the sound of soft breathing, and an occasional scrape of a restless shoe. Through the west windows a flood of sun washed the classroom. Johnny hungered for the streets, his nostrils yearned for fresh air, his legs for movement, his lungs for shouting. . . . Then the bowl of beef stew swam again before his eyes and he sighed.

BRAAAAAAAAANNG! . . .

The gong for closing made Johnny's body jump for joy. A buzz of whispers filled the air and the teacher rapped for order.

"You may pack your books," she said. "And, as each of you pass my desk, stop for your report card." She held aloft a batch of white sheets.

Murmurs of dismay and expectation. Johnny was glad; he wanted his card, for he knew that he had passed. And his mother would be happy when she saw his high marks.

"Pssst!"

2

Johnny turned and saw his pal, Billy, signaling him.

"Wait for me outside," Billy whispered.

"What's up?" Johnny asked.

"Gotta plan to go to the movies," Billy whispered.

"Okie doke," Johnny said.

Wow! His body tingled. The movies . . . maybe Billy had found some money . . .

The teacher rapped her knuckles upon the desk and ordered:

"Rise."

The class struggled to its feet and began to file

out. Standing prim behind her desk, the teacher handed a report card to each pupil as he passed, singing out names:

"Lucy Gerdain . . . Robert Holmes . . . James Dukes . . ."

Johnny inched forward, eager for his card and aching to get out of doors.

"Johnny Gibbs," the teacher sang, handing him his card.

"Thank you, ma'am, " he said.

The teacher smiled at him, crinkling her blue eyes behind thick spectacles. Johnny was scared of her, but her approval made him glow with pleasure. He glanced at his card. A's . . . Yes, A's in every subject. Peaches and cream . . . The world was rosy and he was happy. He jammed the card into his coat pocket, followed the long line into the corridor, through the big door, and down the front steps. About him boys and girls jostled, shouted, and whistled. Jumping Jupiter, he was free until Monday morning. He caught a glimpse of a boy flashing a knife and he smiled superiorly. He had never owned anything but a tiny penknife; nobody ought to bring a big knife like that to school.

But where was Billy? He looked about vainly,

then put two of his fingers in his mouth and blew two loud, short blasts, then a long one. He waited. Then, like an echo, the answer came from his left. He hurried forward. Yes, there was Billy waiting on the corner.

"Hi, Billy. What's up?" Johnny asked.

"My brother Jack's in from the army camp," Billy gushed.

"For real?"

"Yeah. And he's got a gun with 'im."

"You're kidding!"

"The hell I am. Say, you want to go to the movies tonight?"

"Sure. But how?"

"Jack'll take us," Billy explained. "*Superman*'s playing at Loew's State."

Johnny leaped a foot into the air, his eyes glowing. Then he looked crestfallen.

"I've only got thirty cents," Johnny wailed.

"My brother's taking us," Billy said. "He asked me to ask you."

"Wow, man," Johnny approved. "When are we going?"

"Come by the flat at eight," Billy instructed.

"Sure. Fine!"

"So long."

"So long."

They separated, going in opposite directions, their minds filled with Superman. Johnny bubbled with elation. Billy was a good egg, a real pal. He darted homeward through Harlem streets, picturing Superman zooming out of windows, shooting through the sky, moving mountains, lifting up trains, traveling to the moon and back in ten seconds. A cold wind stung his black cheeks and made him turn up his coat collar. Thundering subway trains made the sidewalk quiver under his feet. He elbowed his way through the crowds, hearing a dog bark, a police-man's shrill whistle. Passing a tavern, he heard a jukebox blaring:

I want some seafood, mama . . .

"Hi, Johnny!" a black girl hailed him.

"Hi, Agnes," Johnny answered.

"Can you come over tonight?" Agnes asked.

"Nope," he sang cheerily. "Going to the movies."

"Aw, gee . . . Wish I could go. Say, can't you take me?"

"Not tonight, Agnes," Johnny said, rushing on.

"You could at least stop long enough to say 'Hello, dog!'" Agnes taunted him angrily, poking out her red tongue tip, and flouncing up her dress over her buttocks at him.

His eyes full of his waiting bowl of stew and images of Superman, Johnny sprang upon the stoop of the brownstone tenement in which he lived, pushed open the heavy glass door whose surface was so dimmed by dirty grease that it made the vestibule almost as pitch as night. Clutching the wooden banister, he swung up the steps four at a leap, his stomach crying for his beef stew. Fronting his door, he reached inside his shirt, pulled out the key suspended from his neck by a stout length of twine, inserted it into the lock, turned it, pushed the door in, and stepped into a brightly lit hallway. He paused, his lips parting. The garishly painted yellow walls of the corridor enclosed an alien pile of clutter that he had never seen before. Still as a stone, he blinked at suitcases, trunks, and cartons that blocked his path. What was happening? He had lived in this smelly, ramshackle tenement all his life, but he had never seen the hallway so crowded. Oh, maybe they were moving? Or maybe they had out-of-town visitors? But, no. That big brown suitcase was *his*, the one he had used last summer when he had gone to the boys' camp for his holiday. Then what was it doing sitting here, all packed?

He looked beyond the pile of strange clutter, hearing his mother moving about in the kitchen, rattling dishes, turning the whining water faucet off and on. Barging forward to investigate, he stepped over the trunk and entered the kitchen.

"Hi, Ma," he said. "What's happening?"

His mother was scrubbing a kitchen pan and her big, soft bosom shook as she worked. Then she turned and stared at him with a fleeting smile and he felt all right. Yes, the table was set for him; there was a steaming bowl of . . . No. It was not beef stew; it was ham hock and string beans, which was just as tasty as stew.

"I sure am hungry," he sang.

"Did you wash yet?" his mother asked, her head bent low over the sink.

"No'm. I'll wash in a sec," he said. He was wanting to believe that everything was all right, but that stuff piled up in the hallway worried him. "Ma, what's all that junk in the hallway?"

"Never mind that. You go and wash," his mother directed him.

A hidden note of anxiety in her voice held him still. Why had she glanced at him so quickly and then looked off?

7

"Did somebody come?" he asked.

"Who would be coming?" his mother asked testily.

"Aw, Ma, I want to know, " he begged.

"Will you go and wash?" she asked loudly, glaring suddenly at him.

Her hard black face frightened him. Yes, something was wrong at home. He was torn between the bowl of steaming ham hocks and string beans and the drawn, distressed face of his mother. His tension became so acute that he laughed.

"Somebody's come and you won't tell me," he said airily, leaving the kitchen. As he headed toward the bathroom, he yelled over his shoulder: "I'm going to the movies tonight, Ma."

"You're *what?*" he heard his mother ask in amazement.

He stopped, his mind alarmed at the strange and alien sound in his mother's voice. Shucks, she must be angry at something I did. . . . A moment later he was in the bathroom lathering his hands with a bar of soap; he shut his eyes and massaged his face, hearing his mother's footsteps coming nearer.

"You're going where?" she asked him.

"Billy and his brother are taking me to a movie

tonight," he said matter-of-factly, rinsing his face with warm water and then groping for the towel.

"You can't go to the movies tonight," he heard her say.

"You don't have to worry, Ma," he said, drying his cheeks. "They're paying my way. . . . Say, Ma, look . . ." He pulled his report card from his pocket. "I got all A's this time and—"

"You can't go to the movies tonight." His mother spoke in a cold, quiet tone.

"Why?"

His mouth flew open as his mother walked away. He balled the towel nervously in his hand, wanting to run after her, throw his arms about her, make her melt with love for him . . . What was wrong? Whose baggage was that standing in the hallway? Why didn't she want him to go to the movies? Maybe somebody was sick? Big Sis was sick maybe? Oh, maybe Big Sis was getting married or something? He hung up the towel and strode back into the kitchen.

"Ma, why can't I go to the show tonight?" he asked, sitting automatically at the table and picking up his knife and fork.

"Eat your dinner, Johnny," his mother said.

Her tone made the ham hock and beans lump on

9

his tongue; he stared at her and was about to speak when he heard the front door open. He turned his head, listening to footsteps coming down the hall Yes, that's Big Sis coming from work. Big Sis filled the doorway, but her usually placid face was bleak and tense.

"Hi, Ma," Big Sis said.

"Hello, Sis," his mother said.

"Hi, Sis," Johnny said.

Big Sis glanced guiltily at Johnny and turned away, walking quickly from the kitchen. The wad of food in Johnny's mouth grew too big to swallow; he spat it upon his plate, pushed his chair back from the table, rose.

"What's wrong with everybody?" he asked bawlingly.

His mother began drying her hands hurriedly, her eyes avoiding his. Were they all angry with him because he had done something terribly wrong? Big Sis suddenly reentered the kitchen; the two women now stood staring at each other.

"Sis . . ." his mother began.

"Did you tell 'im, Ma?" Big Sis asked in a waiting, hushed tone.

His mother looked at him, then back at Big Sis.

Then the two women rushed into each other's arms, sobbing fiercely. With numbed fingers Johnny laid his knife down, his hand trembling with alarm. Something was dreadfully wrong and they were hiding it from him. Where was Buddy? Had his brother come home from work yet? Yes, Buddy would tell him what was wrong.

"Where's Buddy?" he demanded of them.

Big Sis dried her eyes and turned to him.

"Buddy came from work and went to Granny's," Big Sis said. "He's eating supper there."

"Why?" Johnny asked. Terror gripped him now. "Where's Pa?"

"Pa's at work, of course," Big Sis said.

"Somebody tell me what's wrong!" Johnny yelled suddenly.

"Now, you don't have to go and get mad," his mother said, her lips trembling.

Big Sis stared at him, her eyes filling with tears; then she rushed once more from the kitchen. Johnny now sensed that whatever was wrong concerned him personally. He stood frozen, looking helplessly at his mother's sobbing.

"Sis," his mother called forlornly.

"Ma, what's the matter?" He touched her shoulder timidly and she pulled away from him, as though he had tried to hurt her.

A sensation of heat played over his skin as he realized clearly now that the things stacked in the hallway were his own. His eyes examined a vacant spot on the kitchen wall where his roller skates usually hung.

"But where's my skates?" he asked singingly, yet knowing that they were packed in the hallway.

Coming again into the kitchen, Big Sis passed him without a glance and Johnny knew that she had done so with effort, that she was on the verge of tears again.

"Stay with me, Sis," his mother sobbed, hugging Big Sis. His mother slowly dried her eyes, her breath heaving in her throat. She stared at Johnny, then looked through the window at the paling winter sky. "Johnny," she began, her tone far away, "I was trying to keep from telling you, child, until you got through with your supper. . . ." She stifled another fit of weeping. "Johnny, you're leaving us tonight."

He felt choked. The room reeled. He made a step toward his mother, then drew back abruptly.

"Leaving?" he echoed. "Why? For where, Ma?"

"Darling, you're . . . going to another home," his mother said.

"But . . . What're you-all talking about? I live here. I'm not going anywhere," his voice came in a hollow whisper. "I'll go only if you're going—"

"Naw. Johnny, you're going to another home tonight. A *good* home. You're going to live with another mother."

"But . . . but you're my mother!" he shouted despairingly. Then he could stand it no longer; his mother's and sister's solid presence seemed unreal; and he ran to them and touched them, with his hands to keep alive in him that this was real, was no dream. But neither of the women looked at him; Big Sis stared out of the window and his mother kept her eyes fixed on the floor, breathing with a groaning sound.

Stunned, he glared at them, then withdrew from them by reflex, in self-defense. His mother and sister had disowned him; they were, therefore, his *enemies*. . . . He backed to the table, his fingers groping for it for support. When Big Sis turned to him, her whole face was a mask of futile love struggling so fiercely against itself that it was really a kind of wild anger.

"Johnny, Ma's not your real mother," Big Sis heaved heavily, still weeping, her lips twisted. "I'm not your real sister. Buddy's not your real brother.

And Pa's not your blood father . . ."

Though the words had come into his ears, they made no sense. He understood the words, but he could not link them with the living moments of his life. Deep in him a cold fury was growing.

"Johnny, did you hear me?" Big Sis asked.

He shook his head and then he too began to cry, silently, looking more baffled than crushed.

"Now, you know," Big Sis said.

"But . . . I'm not going anywhere," he mumbled.

"Tell 'im so he can know, Sis," his mother pleaded.

"You're leaving us tonight," Big Sis stated in an even, neutral manner.

Johnny, before he knew what he was doing, ran at his mother and sister and began raining blows upon them.

"Johnny!" his mother screamed.

"Make 'im stop, Ma!" Big Sis cried.

"Naw, naw, naw!" Johnny wailed as he beat them.

His mother grabbed his shoulders and shook him.

"Stop it, Johnny," she said. "Boy, you got to understand . . ."

As though shocked at himself, he recoiled from

them, glared about the kitchen; he snatched up the bowl of ham hocks and beans and flung it to the floor and stomped his feet into the cushy mess with brutal fury.

"Johnny," Big Sis moaned. "You poor child!"

"Don't talk to me!" Johnny yelled at her.

"Johnny, if you act like that, they won't take you into your new home," his mother warned. "They'll put you in a jail . . ."

Her words struck him stone still.

"What jail?" he asked under his breath. "I've done nothing."

"Johnny, you must stop and listen," Big Sis said. "This is your life, child. Your new mother's coming for you tonight." She sighed. "Listen to us, Johnny. What's happened isn't our fault."

"Johnny, listen," his mother began in a breathless, sighing voice. "I wish I had never to tell you this. I wish I had never let you come to stay with us. The City folks told me not to tell you, and I'll never know why they did it. I obeyed them and kept it from you. I ought to have told you long ago. Last year they said I could tell you, but I couldn't. I loved you too much to tell you, Johnny. I thought they'd let you stay with us till me and Pa died, and then you'd have never known. Sis and Buddy knew about it, but they'd have never told you, 'cause they love you like I do. Son, you see, the City folks came and told me that you had to leave us. They didn't say why. You didn't do anything wrong; nobody's mad at you. It seems that after a child's been in a foster home for a certain number of years, they move 'im to another home. I begged 'em, prayed to 'em, but they said that that was the rule. And there was nothing I could do. They said my home was all right, that you'd done fine here, that you're a real smart boy, but they said you're fifteen years old now and you had to go to a new mother and father."

Johnny' s throat felt hot. Ma was his *mother!* . . .

"Johnny," his mother resumed, "your new mother and father will be all right. They'll be just like we were to you, loving you. . . . You'll see." Her voice fell to a low tone. "You got to believe it, son. Don't let this throw you."

He understood it all now and his eyes were two frozen pools of black stone. He had heard and he had not heard; the words had been too charged for him to sense all that they meant. Only a half hour ago his world had been so solid, real; now he lived in a hot, sick dream. The mother he loved so deeply was now disavowing him, cutting him off, telling him that all his life had been a lie. It was too much; he felt that he was standing in midair and would fall any moment. The kitchen was quiet now save for the musical bubbling of a pot on the stove. Then he ran to his mother and sister and embraced them, sobbing. The two women threw their arms about him, weeping. Then, feeling their quivering arms, he realized that he would never live with them again and he pulled himself free, backing once more to the table. What were they doing to him?

"Don't run from us, Johnny," his mother chided.

He shook his head.

"Darling, rest your head on my shoulder," his mother begged.

"No!" he shouted suddenly.

Big Sis leaned her head against a wall and sobbed.

"You're not my mother," he growled. "You're not my sister."

"Son, don't say that, " his mother pleaded. "I love you."

"It's not our fault, Johnny," Big Sis whimpered.

"Where am I going?" he asked, belligerent and cold now.

"To another nice home, son," his mother said, knotting her fingers.

"You'll have another mother," Big Sis said.

"I didn't ask you!" Johnny screamed at her.

"Don't talk to 'im," his mother warned Big Sis. "Johnny, you haven't done anything wrong. You're bright in school."

"Then why do I have to leave?"

"'Cause the City said so."

"Who is this 'City'?" he asked wonderingly.

"The folks who sent you to live with us when you were a little baby," his mother explained.

"Nobody sent me here," he declared in a wild wail. "If you make me leave, I'll run off!"

"No, Johnny," Big Sis argued gently. "Don't let 'em hear you say a thing like that; they'll put you in a boys' home and—"

"Nobody'll put me anywhere," he hotly disputed Big Sis, trembling all over, afraid of his feelings, for he had never felt this violently before. Then he blinked, trying to grasp it all. "Who did you say wants me to go?"

"The City, son. The folks who take care of orphans," she told him. "Johnny, you have no mother and father. The folks who sent you here said that you've got to leave now . . ."

He tried to move and staggered; he looked again at his mother and then laughed mirthlessly.

"It's not true," he protested feebly. "You're joking . . . I've got a father. Pa's my father. Maybe you're not my mother, but Pa's my pa."

"I'm not your mother and Pa's not your father," his mother said in despair, leaning forward. "Son, I want to help you—"

"That's right," Big Sis joined in. "They didn't give you time to understand all this. Johnny, no matter what they say to you, you're my real brother. I'm your sister. Look, Johnny, when you go to your new home, you can always come to visit us." She smiled through her tears at her mother. "Can't he, Ma?"

"Any time he wants. This is your home, son. No matter where you go, this is home for you," his mother pledged.

"Just pretend you're taking a trip, Johnny," Big Sis suggested. "Then you won't mind it."

"Come here? I'm already here. Why do I have to leave? This is my home . . ." His voice trailed off.

Silence. He saw his mother looking into Big Sis's eyes. Then Big Sis spoke:

"They're coming for you at six o'clock, Johnny, darling. Why don't you eat something?"

Guilt burned in him. Yes, he'd done something wrong and they were getting rid of him. It was a wrong of which they dared not speak. Yes, that was why they'd deliberately sent Buddy away. And they had so arranged it that Pa'd be away too. As he stared at them he felt a new sense of distance; they were rejecting him; he could not look into their eyes and see himself reflected there anymore. And at the same time there was rising in his heart a counterprotective feeling that said: I too reject you. I'll reject you before you reject me. . . .

"Johnny, forgive us, son," his mother prayed. "It wasn't our fault. We didn't want to send you away."

"You're not sending me anywhere," he blurted defiantly, eyes blazing. The thought of the movie flashed through his mind, mockingly. He shook his head.

His mother came slowly toward him.

"Johnny," she crooned, reaching out her hand to him. "You were a little six-month-old baby when you came here. I loved you like you were my own—"

"Where's my mother?" he asked in a whisper, his eyes avoiding hers, dodging her reaching hand.

"I can't tell you that," his mother said.

"How come?"

"The City folks told me not to," his mother said.

"She's dead?" he asked, forcing a desperate note

of hope in his voice.

There was no answer.

"She's dead then," he said with a sigh.

"No," Big Sis said.

"Then where is she?"

"We can't tell you, son."

"You *can*!" he wailed.

"They said that when you're old enough to know, they'd tell you," Big Sis told him.

"And my Pa?"

"We don't know," his mother said.

"Is he dead?"

"We don't know."

"The City folks know?"

"No. They don't know who your father was," Big Sis said.

"Then who knows?"

There was no answer.

"You won't tell me anything," he sobbed, tears scalding his eyes.

"Nobody knows who your father was," his mother whimpered. "Son, maybe someday you'll see your real mother and maybe she'll tell you who your father was. . . ."

"Maybe? Why won't she?" he asked, blinking.

There was no answer.

"My mother . . ." His voice was vague and wondering.

"Son, you've got to be a big man now," his mother said. "You must be brave when they come for you . . ."

Hot hate leaped in him. Who were *they*?

". . . you've just got to go along with 'em. Your new mother's going to love you. We're going to miss you and—"

"I won't miss anybody," he hissed darkly. He looked at the trampled food on the floor, then went to the chair and gripped the back of it with both hands.

"Where are they going to take me?" he asked.

"Right here in Harlem, son," his mother said. "A good lady named Mrs. Green. Just two blocks away."

Then he knew; it was like an illumination: he was not going to the new home. He had not thought it out; that he would not accept a new mother and father declared itself in him . . .

". . . and I'll be visiting you in your new home every day," his mother was saying.

"No," he growled.

"Don't be bitter, son," his mother coaxed.

The doorbell sounded:

22

BRRIIINNNNNNNG!

The two women looked at each other.

"There they are," his mother whispered, her lips breaking into a forced smile. "Let 'em in, Sis. Come on, Johnny, let me help you get fixed up."

"I'll get my coat myself." He waved his mother away, his mind full of the resolution he had made. He swung into the hallway and entered his room and slammed the door shut.

II

Big Sis's footsteps went down the hallway and Johnny heard the front door opening.

"How are you, Mr. and Mrs. Green?" Big Sis was saying. "Come in."

"Hello, Mrs. Gibbs. Miss Gibbs. Is our boy here?"

"He's here."

"Well, since I'm going to be his father, I sure want to see 'im."

"He'll be out in a second. Won't you come into the living room?"

Johnny had listened almost without breathing, his ear glued to the door. Of one thing he was certain: he would not see his new mother and father. He'd find some way of getting shunt of them all . . . He heard them moving slowly down the hall and he jammed his cap on his head, poised to flee. Then he listened.

"Where's he?" Mrs. Green.

"He's in his room, getting his things together." His mother.

"Are these his things here in the hall?" Mr. Green.

"Yes." Big Sis.

"Is he upset about leaving?" Mr. Green.

"Well, you know how it is . . ." His mother. "We're so sorry he's got to leave. He's never known any family but ours. Mrs. Green, why do they want to move 'im after all these years?"

"They just said it was their policy, Mrs. Gibbs. I know it's upsetting you. They had a boy at our home for six years, then they moved 'im. Lord, it broke my heart. In fact, my husband said we'd never take another child. But you get lonely all by yourself and you start remembering that you've got a nice home and there're so many homeless boys and girls in this world. First thing you know, you're asking them to send you a child." Mrs. Green.

"I think it's a shame." Big Sis.

"We sure hate to lose Johnny." His mother.

"By the way, do you know anything about his mother or father?" Mr. Green.

"Shhhhh!"

Trembling, Johnny stood with his ear against the door panel. His right eye twitched and when he lifted his hand to rub it he found tears. He felt encased in hot shame; when they spoke of his mother and father, they whispered. He eased the door open in order to hear better.

". . . he's the best child. He's always at the head of his class. But let me call 'im and he'll show you his report card." His mother.

"Oh, Johnny! Come and meet the folks!" Big Sis.

He stood rigid, fists clenched, unable to answer or move.

"Sis, go and get 'im. Tell 'im his new folks are here." His mother.

Naw, naw . . . He tiptoed down the hallway, scrambled past the trunk, opened the front door, and dashed through it into the corridor, then banged the door behind him. Like lightning, he went down the black stairs and paused, panting at the street door.

"JOHNNY!" Big Sis.

His lips tightened. Yes, he had to run. No one was sending him away; he was leaving of his own accord. He went rapidly to the sidewalk, hearing his mother's and Big Sis's voices echoing:

"JOHNNY! Come back here, you hear!"

Heading down the sidewalk, he reached the subway entrance and ducked into it, glad to disappear, to get out of their way, their reach. He had only thirty cents in his pockets. Well, that was enough to take him away. But where was he going? He only knew that he was fleeing two homes, neither of which he now wanted. Could he go to Billy? He did not know. Who was his friend now? Could he ask Billy for help and trust him not to tell? He was too afraid to do that. He dashed down the subway steps, came to the turnstile, dropped in his fare, pushed through, then stood waiting for a train. He scanned the white and black faces around him, feeling for the first time in his life a certain fear of them. Surely they knew that he was running away. But, no. No one looked at him.

Suddenly what had happened seemed so unreal that he had half a notion to go back. His home tugged at his heart as love and fear fought in him; then he heard a train thundering forward out of the dark. He glanced over his shoulder, searching for the faces of his mother or sister. But only strange faces surrounded him and he felt comforted. Oh, why didn't that train come! If Big Sis came, she'd call on the bystanders to catch and hold him . . . Yes, there was a policeman, but the policeman was not looking at him. Oh, God, let the train come!

Then the two-yellow-eyed train roared screechingly and brutally forward, as wild and violent as the strange news that had greeted him when he had gone home from school. The train stopped and the doors opened. People swarmed off and he pushed past them, grateful for the warmth of the coach. He stood at a window and looked toward the turnstile; no one he knew was in sight. Yes, his mother and Big Sis were no doubt looking for him in the streets, but they'd never, never find him, not as long as they lived.

Yes, he'd take a chance and try to see Billy. He could wait outside of the Loew's State and talk to him. As the train's wheels grated upon steel he thought of his mother, his sister, his brother, his father; well, if he could not have them as his family, then he wanted no family. The station lights that flashed past were like the bowl of ham hock that he did not eat, like the crumpled report card that nestled in his coat pocket, like the *Superman* movie that he'd never see, like Buddy, his brother. . . . They all whisked past in the roar of the subway's dark, alien and unreal.

The strange adults sitting beside and opposite Johnny increased his burden of tension; but, as the train stopped at stations, disgorged its passengers, took on more, and started again, his anxieties abated somewhat. For the first time in his life his sensibilities met the naked reality of the world without an intermediary and his heart pounded. What could he do in this strange world? Where would he sleep? How would he eat? Would it not be wiser to go to that new home? No! He felt that he had been tricked and it was a point of honor with him never to forgive, never to surrender. But, save for a vague hankering to see Billy, he had no plans. And already hunger was gnawing at his vitals.

The train stopped at Forty-second Street and simply because he did not know what else to do, he got off and followed the throngs to the night streets. How huge and real the world was! How like a Christmas tree Times Square looked, with its red and green and yellow and blue lights sparkling against the black sky, yet it all seemed somehow unstable, unreal. He wondered if any of the policemen he saw would challenge him; if they did, he would tell them that he was going to meet his mother who worked . . . Where? Well, he'd make up a story.

His stomach was growling. He bought a bag of hot, buttered popcorn and munched white blooms of salty grain, looking uneasily about. All around him people milled; tall buildings loomed upward into the night, their windows glowing golden. The concrete over which he walked shook from the rush of subway trains. A cold wind was rising. He paused at a street intersection and looked at a manhole cover from which a spout of steam hissed and vanished in the wind.

Passing an office building, he glanced through the glass door into the vestibule; it was empty. He pushed open the door and entered; it was warm and cozy. He leaned against a radiator, chewing the popcorn. What could he do now? Only a dime protected him from hunger. He sighed. Maybe he ought to go to the new home after all? No, no; anything but that . . . He gazed about him in a fit of rebellion.

His eyes fell upon a candy and cigarette stand which was closed and locked. He looked around; the lobby was empty; the elevators were still; the building seemed deserted for the weekend. People were passing the door, but luckily, the candy stand was screened by a corner wall. He tested the lock and found that it would not be difficult to pry off; and beyond the showcase he saw rows and rows of candy bars. His mouth watered. But what if he were caught? Well, what did it matter? He brought out his penknife, looked around. No, no; I can't do this . . . But he was hungry. He pried at the wood, trying to loosen the screws, but the lock would not come off. He hacked with all his strength and the lock clattered to the tile floor and the knife blade sank into the palm of his left hand. A spurt of blood shot out and he clamped his hand to his mouth and sucked the wound. No; he had no time for that. He had to get that candy. He eased down the door and groped inside and began to stuff his pockets with salted peanuts; he felt farther, feeling for the candy. Hard heels tapped past outside. There!

He felt the crinkly paper wrapping the candy bars; he filled his shirt, feeling the crackling paper cold against his skin. He had enough; he had to get out. He went into the vestibule, through the door, and into the streets, hearing the musical noise of the paper wrappings in his shirt. He passed a policeman and held his head stiff until the policeman was out of sight. He pulled out a candy bar and began eating it. He was about to cross the street when a hand fell upon his shoulder.

"Wait a minute, sonny," a voice sounded in his ear.

He turned and looked into the face of the policeman he had just passed. Fear held his body rigid.

"Sir?" he asked breathlessly, flinching, hearing the candy bars rattling.

"What're you doing down here all by yourself, sonny?" the policeman asked, screwing up his eyes.

"I'm meeting my mama," he said, telling his prepared lie.

"Is that true?"

"Yessir. She works late and I always meet her. She's scared to go home by herself," he explained.

"Where does she work?"

"In the Globe movie house, Mister," he said.

"There's no colored woman ushering there," the policeman said.

"She works in the women's washroom," he said.

"Oh! OK, son. Just wanted to see if you were telling the truth," the policeman said, loosening his grip and patting Johnny's head.

Johnny moved on, not daring to look back. When he was a block from the policeman, he ducked down a side street and ran, putting between him and the policeman a hundred thousand people. He began eating another candy bar.

He longed to talk to someone. Yes, he'd risk seeing Billy. What had Billy done when he had not shown up to go to the movies? Billy had no doubt gone to his home and had heard the story of his running away, and perhaps had heard more about his real mother and father than they had told him. Suddenly he did not wish to see Billy, for Billy had become contaminated with the same emotional rejection that he felt toward his mother and father.

But to whom could he talk? There was his teacher, Mrs. Alma Ried, but she was white and she lived somewhere far away. Suppose he telephoned her? No; she'd only call the police . . . But what of his other friends? They'd want to know too much, and they wouldn't be able to help him anyway. And they'd simply feel superior when they learned that he was motherless, fatherless, and had fled his home. They'd make jokes about him.

But he could not tramp the cold streets all night. He had better get back to Harlem. Well, he'd have to walk, for he had not enough money for carfare. Oh, perhaps he could slip into the subway as he had seen other boys do. At 48th Street he went down into the subway; no attendant was on duty and there was a pay turnstile. A woman dropped her fare into the slot and went through. Johnny waited. Finally a young and friendly-looking white man came forward.

"Mister," Johnny called softly.

"What do you want, boy?"

"When you put your fare in, please, let me squeeze through with you," he begged. "I haven't got fare."

"Ha, ha. All right, kid. Come on," the man said.

"Yessir. Thank you, sir."

The man inserted his fare and Johnny squeezed through with him and edged his way past.

"Thank you!" he yelled, running down the platform.

As he waited for the train, he longed to sit down

and think. He'd soon be caught if he kept on this way. The world was proving much harder than he had thought. Every moment presented problems and questions that he could not answer. A Harlem express rolled up; he entered and sat among self-absorbed, warmly dressed adults, white and black, their jaws kneading wads of chewing gum. He got off at One Hundred Twenty-fifth Street and looked bleakly at scenes which would have delighted him only a few hours ago. His world had receded from him, had grown less dependable; yet, at the same time, far more real, distinct, distant but threatening.

Not knowing if he really wanted to see Billy or not, he drifted toward Billy's apartment. Yet Billy remained the only trusted link with the world that had cast him out. He plodded past newsstands arrayed with gaudy periodicals, taverns of milling men and women, drugstores blazing with neon. He slowed opposite the building in which Billy lived. Perhaps his mother or Big Sis had notified the police and maybe some plainclothesman was posted near Billy's to watch for him. He crossed the street and looked at the dark windows of the fourth-floor flat in which Billy lived. Where was Billy? He felt that the world that had known him had forgotten him and was moving on as though he had never existed. Maybe Billy and his family were at his house now? Yes; that was it. Walking in the deep shadows of the buildings, he made his way to his home and looked fearfully up at the lighted windows of his flat. Yes, things were happening there; they were talking of him, pitying him. A policeman came down the block and he ducked into the vestibule and crouched until he had passed. He stood at the glass door and looked dreamily at the yellow streetlamps glowing in the hazy dark. He was hungry, cold, feeling his body growing weaker. If he tried sleeping on the floor behind the stairs, someone might stumble over him. He stiffened; a door behind him opened and a black man came out.

"What're you waiting here for, boy?"

"I live here," he mumbled. "What's it to you?"

"Then why don't you go up to your flat?"

"I'm waiting for my brother," he lied.

The man grunted and left. Would that man tell a policeman that he had seen a boy loitering in the vestibule? Aw, it was too dangerous to lurk here. He wandered again in the direction of Billy's. Oh, God! *Wasn't that Billy there?* Yes, it was! . . . But he dared not call out.

He darted forward, glad that Billy was alone, following Billy until Billy went into an ice cream parlor. Ah, he would talk to Billy now; his heart beat with excitement, for he would learn what had happened at his home since his leaving. Yes, Billy now had his package of ice cream and was on his way out. He closed in on Billy, keeping out of sight, his head hunched against the cold wind.

"Billy," Johnny whispered.

Billy whirled with wide and astonished eyes.

"Johnny," Billy breathed. He smiled, but the smile faded quickly. "They're looking for you. . . ."

"I know it," Johnny said.

"But where've you been? I just came from your house."

"I know. Now, look, Billy . . . I got to talk to you. But don't tell anybody you've seen me, hear? Promise?"

"Er, yes," Billy drawled.

"Billy, I can't go back home," Johnny told him.

"Why?"

"Don't you know? What did they tell you at my house? Say, can't we go somewhere and talk?"

"I got to get this ice cream home," Billy said.

Billy was staring at Johnny with intense interest. Could he trust Billy?

"Let's go into a vestibule and talk," Johnny begged.

"This ice cream's melting," Billy complained.

"Oh, all right," Johnny said with rising anger. "You're my friend, but you're acting like everybody else."

"Aw, no," Billy said. "Look, let me take this ice cream up and I'll slip out and talk to you, hear?" Awe showed in Billy's face. "I know where we can go."

Johnny could not understand the strange glow of admiration that lit Billy's eyes. Would Billy betray him?

38

"You mean that, Billy?"

"Sure! Good God, I want to talk to you too," Billy said and laughed.

"What do you mean?" Johnny asked.

"Gee, I got a lot to tell you," Billy said. "I was at your house when you didn't show up . . ."

"All right. Take the ice cream home. I'll wait for you here," Johnny said.

"OK," Billy said. "Be back in ten minutes."

"But . . . but don't turn me in," Johnny pleaded.

"Trust me," Billy said. "Wait for me, hunh?"

"I'll be waiting," Johnny said. "But if you turn me in, I'll hunt for you as long as I live and I'll kill you, hear?"

Billy stared, nodded, then darted off down the dark sidewalk. Slowly Johnny trailed him, crossed the street, and hid in a doorway. It seemed that he waited a year before he saw Billy reappear, running down the steps, pulling on his overcoat, his eyes gleaming eagerly. He's all right, Johnny told himself with relief.

"Come on," Billy bubbled with excitement. "I know where we can talk."

"Where?" Johnny asked distrustfully.

"It's all right. Follow me," Billy directed.

They walked off, saying nothing. Johnny heard a faint police siren wailing and he clutched Billy's arm.

"It's nothing," Billy said. "Don't be afraid."

They proceeded silently until Johnny saw that they were near the school which both of them attended. Was Billy leading him into a trap?

"Where're we going?" Johnny demanded.

"Follow me, Johnny. You're safe," Billy assured him.

They entered the school grounds. School was closed, so why was Billy bringing him here, if not to trap him for the police? Johnny stopped dead still.

"Billy, what're you doing?" he demanded.

"I know a place," Billy explained. "Trust me. Let's get in first. I'll tell you everything."

They neared the great dark school building,

whose black gleaming windows seemed like a thousand vacant eyes. Billy led Johnny to a window at the basement level, then stooped and hoisted the window up slowly.

"It's not locked, see," Billy whispered. "I've known about this for a long time."

"But what's in here?" Johnny asked.

"Our gang uses this place . . ."

"What gang?"

"I'll tell you about it," Billy said. "Let's get in first and sit down. The moon is coming up and we can sit in a classroom and talk. Ha, ha!"

40

Johnny's anxieties fled. He smiled and clapped Billy on the back.

"I thought you were my friend. Now, I *know* you are," he said.

Billy grinned, looking around to see if they were being observed, then lowered himself through the inky window and then to a concrete floor.

"Come on, quick! We don't want anybody to see this window open," Billy said.

Johnny climbed into the basement and followed Billy forward into darkness. Billy opened a door to a classroom and Johnny paused, staring. Silence was over the rows of desks, the blackboards; only a wall

clock ticked. A faint sheen of moonlight fell from behind a bank of clouds and flooded the windows,
bathing the desks with a ghostly radiance. Billy
laughed.

"It's funny, isn't it?" he asked. "I come here some-
times and just sit down and think . . ." Billy was
silent for a moment, then he continued soberly: "I
don't learn anything in school. I just don't seem able
to catch on to reading and figures. But you're smart,
Johnny."

"What gang is this that comes here, Billy?"
Johnny asked.

"It's a secret," Billy commenced. "We didn't
think you'd ever want to join; that's why we never
told you about it. You never played with the guys in
our block, you know. The gang's been organized a
long time. We call ourselves The Moochers, see? We
had nowhere to meet; one night I saw that the window was broken and I came in and explored the place.
We've got a place rigged up down in the back of the
coal bin. Now, we swap secrets, see. I know yours and
you know mine."

Johnny began to understand his friend's mood.
All along he had known that Billy had been a bad
student, but he had not suspected how deeply Billy

felt about it. Worried about his lessons, Billy had dodged his responsibilities by joining a boys' secret gang.

"Sit down," Billy said, slumping and relaxing behind a desk.

They sat sideways at desks, facing each other, their black faces taut in the bluish glare of moonlight.

"You were at my house," Johnny said tentatively.

Billy's face brightened and Johnny was puzzled. Billy was acting as though some great honor had been conferred upon him.

"Yeah," Billy grinned.

"What did they say about me?"

"They didn't say much," Billy grinned.

"Aw, come on, now," Johnny argued, his anger rising, shame burning his cheeks. "Were those folks there, the Greens?"

"Yeah," Billy said in a happy tone.

Was Billy laughing at his trouble, at his being rejected?

"Hell, you brought me here," Johnny accused. "Now, tell me what they said. Why did the City folks want me to leave my home?"

"Don't you know really?" Billy asked in amazement.

42

"I wouldn't be asking you if I did," Johnny growled.

"You're kidding," Billy taunted, laughing lazily.

"Don't tease me, Billy," Johnny wailed angrily. "You've got a mother and a father and a home and—"

"Gee!" Billy cut him off. "Johnny, I wish to God I was you!"

Johnny blinked and stared. Billy had sounded sincere, serious; but why?

"What the hell do you mean?"

"God, I wish somebody would drive me from home," Billy wailed plaintively.

Speechless, Johnny gaped. Never had he thought that he would meet someone who would envy him his plight!

"You don't understand, Billy," Johnny reasoned patiently. "Do you know why they wanted to send me to another home? They said I don't belong there. They said that they are not *my* mother and father . . ."

Billy's eyes glowed with envy and jealousy. He was proud of Johnny! He thought that what had happened to Johnny was something great!

"Billy, don't be a fool!" Johnny blurted, anger almost choking him. "Now, what did they say?"

"They said a lot of things," Billy spoke slowly. "But I didn't understand it all and—"

"The hell you didn't!" Johnny raged. "Tell me. No matter what it was."

"Johnny, what's the matter?" Billy asked. He now was puzzled. "I've never seen you act like this before."

"Well, tell me what they said!" Johnny shouted in a frenzy.

"Sh! Not so loud," Billy cautioned. "People might hear us in here."

Johnny sobered; he settled back and glowered at the bleak and shadowy walls.

"Help me, man!" Johnny was guttural. "Can't you see I've no place to go?" He trembled, clenched his fists, angry at Billy because Billy knew more about him than he did. Suspicion cropped up again against Billy. But what could Billy gain by betraying him?

"Well," Billy began, "they were all crying. And my brother and I kept asking 'em what was the matter, where you were, and then they said that you'd run off."

"I know that," Johnny was savage. "But what else?"

"They said they wanted you to go to a new home and—"

"I KNOW ALL THAT!" Johnny shouted peevishly. "I want to know . . ." His voice trailed off.

"What?" Billy asked.

"Did they say anything about my *real* mother and father?" Johnny asked.

"Oh, that . . . Naw, not much. Ha, ha! Naw, they're not your *real* mother and father."

"Did they say who my real mother and father were?"

"Er . . . Yeah. They talked about 'em," Billy mumbled.

"Well, who are they?" Johnny demanded desperately.

Johnny trembled. Billy looked frightened. Johnny felt maddened, for he realized that Billy regarded him as a kind of hero and could not understand his frenzied anxiety. Or was Billy slyly trying to evade telling him the awful truth about his real mother and father?

"You see, Johnny," Billy began humbly, "they used some big words I didn't understand, but I'll tell you what I heard, see? Well, it seems that your mama went down to Atlantic City—"

"When? Where is she now?" Johnny demanded.

"I don't know," Billy said evasively. "I'm talking about something that happened before you were born . . ."

"Oh!"

"She met a man there . . ."

"Well, go on."

"Gee, I don't know," Billy faltered. "It seems like she met this man and they got drunk. I don't know . . ." Billy broke off in confusion. "Gee, Johnny, I'm only saying what they said, see? Seems like she got drunk and the man gave you to her . . ." Billy frowned. "Say, Johnny, do people have babies when they get drunk?"

"I don't know," Johnny confessed in despair.

"You read a lot of books, Johnny," Billy charged. "You ought to know."

"There're no books in the library about things like that," Johnny mumbled sullenly.

"Oh, I remember," Billy exclaimed. "They said you were conceived that night. I don't know what that means, but it is the word they used. They said your mother only stayed with the man one night. Then your mother went back to Harlem and—"

"With my father?" Johnny asked hopefully.

"Naw," Billy drawled; he was out in water above his head now. "Seems he just left her, didn't want to marry her."

"Why?"

"Don't know. Some men just don't want to marry

women," Billy tried to explain. "And seems like she didn't even remember your father's name . . . Oh, Johnny, I don't remember all they said. But they weren't married, like my old man is married to my old woman, or like Mr. Gibbs is married to Mrs. Gibbs."

Johnny winced, unable to look at Billy now, his mind teeming with images of shame and degradation.

"What did my father do then?" he asked slowly.

"I don't know," Billy said. "Seems that that was the only time your mama saw your papa. Seems like they didn't know each other enough to get married."

Johnny turned away as hot tears coursed on his black cheeks.

"And what did my mother do then?" he asked in a choked voice.

"Well, they said that she was sick here in Harlem," Billy went on in a neutral, businesslike tone.

"And where was I?"

"You . . . ?" Billy paused, then laughed. "Hell, you weren't even born then. You were in her stomach, where they say babies sleep before they are born."

"And then what happened?"

"Then your mother was awfully sick," Billy told him again.

"What kind of sickness?"

"I don't remember the name of it."

"Where was she sick? Her heart? Her . . . her . . ."

"The sickness was in her head," Billy related. "That's what they said. They said she had *demon* . . . *demon* something. I can't remember. There was another word. Sounded like tea or something. Oh, yes. They said it was *demon preco* or something like that."

"It was in her head?"

"Yeah."

"Is it something bad?"

"I don't know, Johnny," Billy said. "But when you got it, it seems like you don't know what you're doing when you do something. Like crazy folks act, see?"

Johnny shuddered, then bared his teeth in the dark gloom.

"My mother was a crazy woman?" Johnny asked disbelievingly.

"That's what they said, Johnny," Billy explained.

Johnny felt that he wanted to leap at Billy and lash his fists into his face, yet he knew that Billy was innocent.

"And where was I then?" he asked Billy.

"You were still in her stomach," Billy explained.

"She still had that *demon preco* in her head, see? That's all that happened."

"What do you mean? That couldn't be all you heard."

"Well, it seems that they put your mother in a . . . put her away. You know. In one of those asylums," Billy related.

"Where is she now?"

"It seems like she's still there," Billy said. "They said they never wanted to tell you, because it would make you sad. Say, Johnny, you didn't know anything about this until now?"

"Nothing," Johnny sighed.

Johnny fell to mulling over the story that had been kept from him. That was his past. And that dim, wild woman was his mother. And a man without a face or a name was his father.

". . . Mrs. Gibbs said that you ought to know your mother now," Billy was saying. "She said that you ought to go and see her now. She said that you were old enough."

"I'm not going to see her," Johnny spoke with bitter anger.

"Why?"

"She's not my mother . . ."

"Yes; she is."

"Hell, naw! She's not! A woman crazy in the head? Hell, naw!"

"Gee, I don't know, Johnny."

"What did they say happened to my father?" Johnny asked.

"Well, seems like when your mother had that *demon preco* she couldn't tell anybody who your father was, see," Billy said. "She couldn't remember. They said she was asked over and over again, but she just couldn't remember. Nobody ever found your father. But, shucks, that's nothing. You'll find 'im some day."

"For what?"

"Hunh, Johnny?"

"Nothing."

"Gee, Johnny, I wish to God I was you!" Billy exploded again in a psalm of jealousy. "You don't have to go to school now. Honest to God, I wish something like that had happened to me!"

"Billy, you're crazy!"

"Naw, I'm not. That's why I joined this gang. Wait until you meet 'em. They'll like you. You just tell 'em what I told you and they'll take you in. Feed you. Find a place for you to sleep. Get you some clothes, everything . . . But me? Shucks, my old man just gets drunk every night and beats me, my sister, and my ma. That's why I stay away from home all the time. But if I had no ma and no pa, that'd be easy. All you've got to do is dodge the police. Gee, Johnny, you're a man now. You can do what you want. Go where you please. You're tall and folks'll take you for a grown-up. Say, you can get you a girl now. Say, Johnny, if you do, will you promise to tell me all about it, how it makes you feel? They say it's something out of this world. Holy cats, you can even get married, just like a real man!"

"Hush, Billy," Johnny half moaned. "You're talking crazy."

"Say, I'm going to run away with you, hunh?"

"Naw. You stay home."

"I'm almost as old as you."

"Naw! I don't want you with me."

"Then you plan to go to that new home?"

"Naw!"

"Then you're going to join The Moochers?"

Johnny did not reply. He realized that he had no choice. What was the use in finding his crazy mother? His old mother and father had disowned him. And he did not want a new family. He felt like a block of ice. He had been hoping against hope that some other story would have been given him about his origins, and now he had the bleakest and most shameful origin possible. He was nothing, a nobody; he felt that he had no claim upon anybody in the world. The feeling of estrangement that had set in when his mother and sister had told him that he was to go to a new home now draped him like a black cowl; it was a feeling that was to remain with him all his life, a feeling out of which he was to act and live, a feeling that would stay with him so long that he would eventually forget that it was in him. He roused himself and heard Billy speaking:

". . . the hideout's downstairs, behind the furnace. They'll show it to you. I took an oath not to tell anybody, but since you're not going back home, I'll tell the gang to take you in, see?" Billy explained. "You'll be safe with 'em. I got to go, but I'll write a note. You just give it to 'em and they'll feed you and let you sleep here."

"OK," Johnny agreed listlessly.

Billy went to the front of the classroom and rummaged in a teacher's desk and returned with pencil and paper and, by the light of the pale moon, he scribbled a note. At the bottom of the page he drew a

crude skull and crossbones, then added several mysterious symbols.

"What's that?" Johnny asked.

"I can't tell you that," Billy mumbled solemnly.
"It's our secret code. If I didn't put it here, they'd kill
you sure. . . ."

Johnny laughed and Billy looked up, amazed.

"I'm not kidding you, Johnny," Billy said.

"But what would they kill me for?" Johnny
asked.

"Look, Johnny, don't you play these fellows
cheap," Billy cautioned. "They mean business. The
cops want most of 'em. They don't go to school; they
live by snatching and mugging, see? They sleep days
and hunt at night. If you don't act right, they'll rub
you out. I mean it."

Johnny blinked. Yes, Billy was serious. This was a
new Billy, not the smiling Billy he had always
known.

"I understand," he told his friend.

"You better," Billy warned. "And do what they
tell you." Billy sighed. "God, I wish I could stay."
His voice grew soft. "If the gang takes you in, they'll
tell you everything." Billy shook his finger in
Johnny's face. "But they'll have to test you first."

"How?"

"I can't tell you that," Billy mumbled. "But they'll like you. You know a lot of things that they want to know."

"How am I going to meet them?"

"You just stand there, right by that window," Billy instructed him. "Don't move from there. When they come through, around midnight, just give 'em this note. Baldy is the leader."

"Who?"

"Baldy. A guy with a bald head . . ."

"But you just said that they were boys like me."

"They are. But the leader is bald-headed. He's a boy," Billy said. "You'll learn. But, let me tell you one thing: don't ask too many questions. They don't like that. Just hang around and they'll tell you everything."

"Billy, if this is a double cross, I'll kill you," Johnny swore.

"I'm straight," Billy pledged, folding the note and stuffing it into Johnny's hand. "Don't let anybody see it but the gang. If the police come, chew it and swallow it, see?"

"OK."

"I got to go," Billy said, leading the way back to

the basement-level window. Johnny stood in the gloom as Billy lifted the window slowly. Billy turned and stared at Johnny with sad but eager eyes, then he scrambled out and said: "God, I wish I was you." Billy pulled the window shut.

IV

Through the windowpane, Johnny watched his friend vanish into the night. Then he felt scared; he was alone now. He had accepted being on his own. He would now have a new home, a home that would be different from that of Mr. and Mrs. Gibbs, or that of Mr. and Mrs. Green. He sighed, hearing the wind blow steadily through the school yard. From outside came a faint shrill whistle. Then a mysterious creak sounded somewhere in the dark depths of the building. Terror seized him and he grew wet with sweat, a sweat that clung to the crinkly paper wrappings of the candy bars in his shirt. He thought of removing the candy, but he simply did not have strength enough. Fighting against sensations that sought to claim him, he moved nervously and the note in his hand rattled with a dry and ominous whisper. Yes, this was his passport to his new life, to the new and strange gang of boys upon whom he would have to depend for his food, for friendship. If, for any reason, they rejected him, he would be once again upon the cold, windswept streets. In spite of himself, his mind drifted toward that mother of his that he could not remember, a mother who was mindless and in a cell; he did not know her and she did not know him. Suddenly he felt that he was guilty of some great and awful but nameless wrong. He leaned forward and sobbed with a quivering throat.

57

Then he was still for a long time, filled with a strange sense of void; yet, there was rising up in him, out of the debacle of his former feelings, a new self and, when he became aware of that self, it was already firmly lodged in his mind and heart. He had to survive, had to be hard, had to watch, had to plot and plan, had to study each person he met, had to weigh the value of each hour of the day; there were times when he would have to be passive, when he would have to act and strike without warning.

Long past midnight he heard what seemed a cautious footstep in the gravel outside of the window.

Though he knew that the sound signaled the approach of the gang, he shrank tensely into the shadows of the corridor. Slowly, silently, the window was hoisted about a foot. Did they suspect his presence? Then he heard:

"Come on. All's clear."

The window went all the way up and a dark form climbed through and landed on the floor; another came, then still another. He wanted to make his presence known, but he waited. When all three of the forms were in the corridor, the window was shut. Johnny now stepped forward, cleared his throat to announce himself. In the dark shadows he extended the white blur of notepaper.

"Say," he began, "Billy told me—"

He never finished the sentence. There was a swift scuffling of feet; the blade of a knife flashed before his eyes and hard hands pinned him brutally against a wall. He gave a grunt as a knee thundered into his stomach and a hard hand was clamped tight over his mouth.

"One sound and we'll kill you, you bastard," a rasping voice said.

Johnny held still, breathing in deep gasps.

"Hold the flashlight on his face," somebody ordered.

Johnny's eyes were blinded with light. He tried to make out the faces beyond the cone of light, but could not.

"Who in hell are you, Bo?" a hissing voice asked.

"I—I got a note," he managed to say.

"Talk fast, bastard," somebody muttered as though his explanation had been valueless.

"The note . . . it's in my hand," he panted. "Billy gave it to me."

"What Billy?" somebody asked insistently. "What in hell do you know about us?"

"Who is he, Baldy?" a voice asked.

"I'll be damned if I know," the rasping voice replied.

"Here's the note," Johnny said again.

"What goddamn note?" the harsh voice asked again.

"R-r-right here," Johnny said.

They relaxed their hold upon him now. The knife blade felt cold and sharp where it rested against the skin of his throat.

"What's he saying, Baldy?" somebody asked.

"I don't know what the hell he's talking about," the voice near him snarled.

"The n-note . . . it's h-here in my hand," Johnny breathed, realizing that he had to make them understand. "Take the note . . . and read it. Billy gave it to me. Billy Sayers. You know 'im. He was here a little while ago." His husky voice died away.

"How do you know about Billy?" a demand came out of the dark.

"R-read the n-note," he pleaded desperately.

His eyes had become accustomed to the flash-light's glare and he could see doubt and fear on their faces.

"Skinkie, take that note," a voice directed. "Give it to Baldy."

Johnny now recognized the boy called Baldy. In the moonlight a bald head gleamed dully in front of him, a bald head that had a young face; and it was this Baldy who had the rasping voice, who was hold-ing the knife at his throat and a knee in his stomach. Baldy's face was tight, black, hard, brutal, with red eyes and swollen lids. The thin, dry lips were slightly parted and Johnny could see short, stubby white teeth.

Skinkie, a boy with a round, brown face, large black eyes, fat lips that dropped flabbily down, came forward and snatched the note from Johnny's fingers and stepped cautiously away and opened it, holding the flashlight to it.

"What does it say?" Baldy asked, holding the knife blade steady against Johnny's throat.

"It's from Billy all right," Skinkie mumbled, "'cause here's the code."

"Give it here," Baldy said. He took his knee from Johnny's stomach, snatched the note from Skinkie, but still held the knife blade against Johnny's throat.

The other two boys released their hold upon Johnny, but Baldy, taking no chances, muttered:

"Watch that sonofabitch!"

Quickly Johnny's arms were pinioned again.

"Stand still, Bo," Skinkie warned. "I've got an ice pick right here at your heart. If it goes in, what'll come out won't be catsup."

"OK," Johnny breathed.

Baldy read the note and passed it on to the others.

"He must be all right," Baldy said in a relenting tone. He came close to Johnny. "But if you're stooling us, Bo, we'll kill you, see?"

"I'm not stooling," Johnny said.

"All right," Baldy snapped. "Take 'im to the hole." Baldy paused. "Put blinkers on 'im, Skinkie."

"Give me your handkerchief," Skinkie asked of the third boy.

A boy whom Johnny had not seen clearly came

61

forward out of the shadows and thrust a dirty handkerchief across Johnny's eyes and tied it in a knot at
the back of his head. Then he felt the sharp jab of the
tip of the ice pick at his spine.

"Walk ahead, slowly," Baldy directed. "Watch
your step."

"One false move," Skinkie warned, "and I'll push
it through to your goddamn navel."

"I'll do what you say," Johnny whispered his obe-
dience.

"You're goddamn right you will," Baldy grunted
sadistically.

Johnny moved forward into pitch blackness,
dragging his feet for fear he would encounter steps or
a wall, hearing the other boys whispering behind
him, feeling the ice pick tip touching the naked skin
of his spine.

"I can't see," he complained softly.

"You just walk and we'll tell you what to do,"
Baldy was sarcastic. "We'll tell you when to breathe,
you sonofabitch."

"I'll do everything you say," Johnny pledged himself helplessly.

"You'd better," Baldy jeered.

Johnny moved forward for two minutes and then
heard Baldy say:

"Stop, Bo! OK, Skinkie, get that door open."

Johnny heard footsteps running ahead and a second later there came the sound of a lock clicking and a door swinging on rusty hinges.

"OK, Bo," Baldy said. "There're steps here. Go down slowly. Goddammit, if you fall, you'll break your goddamn neck."

Johnny descended the steps as though walking through a great tide of water.

"What're we going to do with this sonofabitch?" a voice asked.

"We're going to find out about 'im," Baldy said. A moment later he snapped: "Here's the bottom, Bo. Watch it."

63

Johnny felt the floor with his foot and halted; he knew that he was standing on a gritty surface, a floor of coal dust or ashes. An airy, clean smell filled his nostrils. The ice pick left his spine and he heard the knife click shut. Then both of his arms were once more pinioned and he was led slowly forward. They stopped; another door was opened; again Johnny went forward into blackness. Then he was pushed roughly forward into space.

"Get in!" Baldy shouted.

Johnny stumbled over his own feet and then stood still.

"Shut the door, Treetop," Baldy ordered.

A door banged.

"Give me a match," Skinkie said.

Johnny heard a match scratching to flame and, at the same time, Baldy tore the blindfold off his eyes. Skinkie was busy lighting four half-burned candles that stood upon an overturned, empty packing box. The dirty room, which stood beside a coal bin, was about twelve feet by twenty and was filled with old desks, boxes of chalk, blackboards, and sealed paper cartons. Baldy pushed Johnny toward an old desk.

"Sit down, Bo, and let's lamp that puss of yours," Baldy growled.

Johnny sank down upon the desk and looked fully into the faces of his captors. There was Baldy, squat, black, thick; his face was narrow and the crown of his head was a shining dome. Though Johnny knew that Baldy was the leader of the gang, he felt a desire to laugh at the old man's head capping the child's face. How had Baldy got like that?

And there was Skinkie, with his round face and large, limpid eyes. He did not like Skinkie, for the boy's bloodshot eyes hinted at cruelty and a mysterious reserve of brute strength.

Treetop was a tall, muddy-colored mulatto boy

with coal-black, straight hair; his skin was dotted with pimples, many of which ran with watery matter. Thin as a rail, Treetop was a head taller than the others and he kept his full lips tightly shut. Johnny sensed in him a terrible intensity and he found that he could not look Treetop in the eyes for long.

"What they want you for?" Treetop asked.

"Who?" Johnny asked.

Baldy reached out the flat palm of his right hand and slapped Johnny across the face, making his head snap back and stars dance before his eyes. Pain numbed his lips and he tasted the warmth of his own blood.

"When you hear a question, you answer, you sonofabitch," Baldy snapped.

"I don't know what you mean." Johnny hummed with anger.

"What do the cops want you for?" Baldy demanded.

"Nothing," Johnny answered.

"Then what the hell are you here for?" Baldy asked.

Johnny sighed and leaned forward. These were hard boys.

"Didn't Billy tell you in the note?" he asked.

Baldy grasped a handful of hair on the top of Johnny's head and rammed Johnny's face backward.

"Stop stalling, you bastard," Baldy snarled. "When we ask you a question, answer!"

"I—I r-ran away from home," Johnny gasped.

"Why didn't you say that in the first place?" Treetop demanded.

Johnny did not answer. Yes, he had to be on his toes here, had to watch every word he uttered, or else incur some terrible penalty.

"What'd you take a powder for?" Skinkie asked.

"Why did I run off?" Johnny asked with echoes in his voice.

"Yeah. Why'd you run off?" Baldy sneered with deriding patience.

"The City sent me to live with a family when I was about six months old," Johnny spoke hurriedly. "I thought they were my real folks all the time, see? But today they told me they weren't, that I had to leave and live with another family. So I ran away."

"Oh, so you're a moocher, hunh?" Baldy asked.

"W-what's a m-moocher?" Johnny asked.

"Ha, ha. Looks like you don't know beans, do you?" Baldy asked in a wondering tone, a tone holding a contemptuous kindness. "What's your handle?"

"Johnny Gibbs."

"Hunh-hunh. We'll give you another name," Baldy said.

"Why?"

"You'll learn. We're The Moochers, see? You're a Moocher too. Billy sent you to the right hole, all right. We used to live in foster homes too. We had sense enough to get out," Baldy explained.

Skinkie and Treetop laughed. Baldy walked in a circle, scratching his hairless head.

"Goddamn, you're sure dumb," Baldy commented. "In that note Billy said that you were smart, but you don't act a damn bit like it."

"I'm an orphan," Johnny said. "But I didn't know it until today."

"From here out, you'd better start knowing things." Baldy laid down the law of gang life.

"Aw, give the jerk a chance," Skinkie suggested, grinning.

"We all got to learn some way," Treetop muttered.

"You won't be any good to this gang if you always think as slow as you're thinking tonight, dope," Baldy explained kindly. "Maybe you're smart to the teachers in this school. But we can't use school shit."

Baldy giggled. "We don't want snotty noses in this gang. Dopes are dangerous not only to themselves, but to us, see? We're tough, kid. It's what you've got up here that counts," Baldy said, tapping his slick skull.

Treetop was watching Johnny with an indulgent smile. Skinkie was sitting on the edge of the packing box, near the burning candles, swinging his legs. For some odd reason Skinkie was holding his fingertips over the hot flame of the candles, taking them away each time just when his skin began to feel the heat. For a while there was silence. Johnny stared at Baldy, fascinated by the contrast between the young face and the bald head.

"You got a tomato for yourself?" Treetop asked.

"What's that?" Johnny asked.

"A gal, a dame, a hole, a broad," Treetop explained softly. "A tomato is something that you squeeze to get hot juice out of."

"Naw. I haven't got a girl," Johnny said.

"Who do you know besides Billy?" Baldy asked.

"Nobody . . . just the guys in my class," Johnny said.

"I don't think we ought to do anything tonight," Treetop told Baldy.

"I'll handle that," Baldy said, turning belligerently to Treetop. "I'm in control here. Now, here's a job for you. Get over to Billy's and check on this Bo's story, see? Make it snappy. If what Billy says is true, we'll work tonight. We'll break this bastard in."

"OK. You're the boss," Treetop agreed, rising and leaving.

Again there was silence. Skinkie and Baldy took paper bags from their pockets and lined them up on the packing box. Johnny knew that the food had been stolen, for nothing was properly wrapped. There was a long piece of cooked ham, a loaf of sliced bread, and several bottles of soda pop. Baldy and Skinkie pulled up desks and began to eat.

"You hungry, Bo?" Baldy asked, glancing at Johnny.

"Yeah. I'm kind of hungry," Johnny mumbled meekly, yearning for the taste of meat in his mouth. "Say, I got some candy bars here . . ."

He reached inside of his shirt to get the candy; there was a quick, general movement from Baldy and Skinkie. The two boys sprang across the gritty floor and flung themselves upon Johnny before he could take his hand out of his shirt.

"Naw, you don't, you goddamn sonofabitch," Baldy hissed.

"Drop it! Drop it!" Skinkie was screaming.

Johnny was thrown back to the dusty ground; he

wilted in terror, not knowing what was happening.

"What's the m-matter?" Johnny gasped.

With heaving chests, Baldy and Skinkie ripped off Johnny's coat, then his sweater, and finally his shirt. The candy bars spilled to the floor.

"Well, I'll be goddamned!" Baldy breathed.

"You poor dumb cluck," Skinkie simpered.

"Where'd ya get 'em from, dope?" Baldy asked, picking up bars.

Johnny understood now. They had thought that he was reaching for a weapon.

"I took 'em out of a showcase down in Times Square," Johnny told them.

"Gee, you're not so dumb after all," Skinkie allowed himself to say.

"Well, guy, you're sure lucky," Baldy said, lining the candy bars up on the packing box. "Look, don't ever do that again. You're crazy. Wrong moves like you made have cost dopes their lives. If you had taken your hand from your shirt before I grabbed you, you would've been a goner." Baldy pulled a .32 from his hip pocket and waved it. "I almost used it. But I just took a chance to see what you had." He looked pityingly at Johnny and shook his head. "Come on here to the box and eat something, you crazy sonofabitch."

Johnny sighed, relaxed, and sat at the improvised table. Now they seemed, after having almost killed him, on the verge of accepting him; yet he knew that the final word depended upon what Treetop brought back from Billy. He munched, staring moodily at the flaring candle flames. Baldy opened a bottle of pop with his teeth and gurgled down half of it. Johnny wanted them to like him, to trust him. Again he studied Baldy's slick head, which reflected the candlelight like water at night under a bright moon. He had a desire to laugh, and, before he knew it, he was asking:

"How old are you, Baldy?"

Baldy stopped chewing and glared at him.

"What's that to you?"

Skinkie snickered, but stopped quickly. Tension stood in the air. Skinkie stopped chewing and stared from Baldy to Johnny. Johnny smiled, trying to convey to Baldy his goodwill.

"I was just wondering how you lost your hair," Johnny said. "You don't look old enough to be bald yet."

Baldy's fist shot forward, smashing Johnny between the eyes, sending him toppling back upon the floor, his head banging against the ashes and coal dust, a flash of white flicking before his eyes. Too late he realized that he had uttered the tabooed words. Teeth bared, Baldy loomed over him.

"Stand up, Bo!" Baldy ordered. "I'm going to teach your ass a lesson!"

"I don't want to fight," Johnny said. "I didn't mean to say—"

Baldy stooped and grabbed Johnny and yanked him to his feet.

"You either fight me or I'll kill you," Baldy roared.

Johnny knocked Baldy's hand from his shirt collar; he was so angry now that he had no thought of danger. Baldy landed a hard right on Johnny's cheek. Johnny ducked away, his guard up. Baldy crowded in, lashing out with another right, but Johnny ducked it. Johnny knew now that the fight was being forced upon him, that nothing he could do would make amends. He danced out of range as Baldy threw another right, never letting up for a second. Baldy rushed yet again and Johnny clenched; the force of Baldy' s charge sent Johnny crashing back into the empty packing box, tumbling it. The ham, bread, candy, and soda pop bottles clattered to the floor; the candles flickered out as they fell, plunging the room into darkness.

"Get those candles lit!" Baldy cried.

"Just a sec," Skinkie muttered.

"Quick!" Baldy yelled. "I'm going to kill this sonofabitch!"

Johnny was resolved to fight now. He could not be a member of this gang if Baldy could feel that he was one who could be slapped about at will. A match exploded into flame and Skinkie lit a candle, then held the lit candle to the others. Johnny could sense Skinkie's hysterical eagerness to see the fight. Baldy, his bare head tucked turtlelike into his shoulders, circled him, then sent a pile-driving blow to the right cheek of Johnny. Johnny shook his head, his watchful eyes waiting for an opening, crouching. Yes, he would fight to the end if necessary.

"I'm going to knock you cold, you bastard," Baldy vowed. "Do you want to stand still and let me clip you, or do you want to fight?"

Johnny said nothing.

"You're asking for it, you dumb sonofabitch," Baldy sneered.

Skinkie watched with a tight smile, a neutral smile. Johnny sensed that the floor was slippery now, littered with bits of ham, shards of broken soda pop bottles, and soggy slices of bread trampled into coal dust. Johnny suddenly knew Skinkie's mood; Skinkie wanted to see Baldy beaten. Maybe Treetop did too. Yes, this was his test. Then, like lightning, Baldy ducked and flung himself forward, tackling Johnny about the knees, toppling him. Goddamn! He should have been on the lookout for a trick like that. Before he could regain his breath, he felt Baldy's fingers digging themselves into his throat. Johnny let out a scream of rage, heaved up his stomach with all of his strength, and tossed Baldy off him. Both scrambled to their feet. Baldy cursed under his breath and Johnny heard a gasp of surprise from Skinkie. Baldy rushed again, swinging a right against Johnny's jaw, staggering him.

"You beast!" Johnny yelled.

Baldy came in again, machinelike, and landed a right into Johnny's stomach. Johnny grunted and clenched. They whirled about the room, their arms locked about each other's necks, gasping and grunting from exertion. Baldy broke free. Johnny now stooped quickly and grabbed Baldy about the knees and, with one supreme act of physical will, lifted the bald-headed body high into the air and flung it back to the floor. Baldy's body landed with a thud, actually bouncing slightly.

"Look!" Skinkie screamed excitedly. "God Almighty!"

Panting curses, Baldy began weeping, his face drenched in sweat, his bald dome dirty with coal dust and ashes. Baldy struggled to his feet and charged in wild anger. Johnny backed off, then slowly lifted his right foot, the toe of which was hard and sharp, and held it ready. As Baldy closed in, Johnny swung his foot high, aiming at Baldy's chin, the muscles of his legs flexed. The shoe met Baldy's chin bone, sounding like a rifle shot, sending Baldy's head back as though some steel wire had jerked it. Baldy slid to the floor, limp, groaning in semiconsciousness, his lips slobbering foam and blood. Dazed, Baldy rose, leaned forward, and screamed:

"I'm the leader man of this gang! For that kick, I'm going to beat your brains out!"

Baldy looked about quickly, spying a rusty knife blade on the gritty floor. He swooped and grabbed it, straightened, and lunged at Johnny. Johnny backed off, then leaped behind the overturned packing box for protection. He desperately yearned to hold a counterweapon in his hands, but what? There flashed through his mind the pieces of broken bottle that littered the floor. Yes, there was a bottle near his right foot. He could do as much harm with that bottle as Baldy could with the knife. He bent his knees and scooped up the bottle, holding it by the neck,

75

pointing the jagged edges toward Baldy's face, ready to fight on an equal plane now.

"Goddamn, goddamn," Skinkie sang in awe.

"If you cut me, I'll cut you," Johnny vowed.

"Then we'll die right here," Baldy accepted the challenge.

Johnny saw that Baldy was a bit hesitant now, knew that he was thinking of his position of leader man of the gang, knew that Baldy was dangerously desperate. Baldy rushed, but Johnny kept the packing box between them. Baldy pursed his lips and spat into Johnny's face.

"Come on and fight," Baldy snarled.

Johnny wiped the spittle out of his eyes; he was enraged, but knew that it was better to keep cool. He yearned to fling himself upon that hateful, bald-headed boy and slash his face to ribbons, but he feared that rusty, poised knife.

"I'll pay you for kicking me if I have to go to hell," Baldy hummed.

"I'll pay you for spitting on me if I die," Johnny countered.

Johnny wanted it over now; cautiously, he came out from behind the box, taking the bottle from his right hand and holding it in his left, wanting to keep his right hand free to fend off Baldy's attack with the knife. Baldy grinned with swollen and bloody lips.

"Come on; come on," he baited Johnny.

"Jesus Christ," Skinkie sang.

Johnny advanced slowly, holding the sharp, jagged edge of the bottle in his left hand, his right hand ready to dart forward and catch Baldy's right hand. He held his left hand high, aiming at Baldy's face, his eyes, hoping that a slash would send blood to blind Baldy's sight. Baldy backed off now, sensing danger. Tensed, they held still, their breaths heaving slow and deep. Johnny mapped a plan of action; he feinted. Baldy leaped backward. Johnny smiled, wanting Baldy to relax for one split second.

"You're scared of me, Baldy?" he taunted.

Baldy raged, grinding his teeth, aching to leap forward with the knife, but afraid of that icy edge of broken glass. Johnny advanced and Baldy backed away until his shoulders touched the wall behind him.

"You can't run any farther, Baldy," Skinkie mumbled.

"He's scared," Johnny said, forcing a laugh.

It was more than Baldy could take; he leaped forward, throwing caution to the winds, swinging down his right arm, the knife blade headed for Johnny's chest. Johnny quickly dropped the broken bottle and lunged forward, both of his hands grappling for Baldy's right arm. He found it and hung on for dear life. He felt free, almost triumphant, for that knife was no longer now pointing at his heart. It was now a test of his strength against Baldy's. Baldy's knee came into his stomach but he still clung to that right hand clutching the knife. Again Baldy kneed Johnny, trying to shake Johnny loose, but Johnny hung on. Then he twisted Baldy's right arm, carrying it backward like a chicken wing. Baldy screamed with pain and dropped to the floor, but his right hand still clutched the knife. Johnny went down with him, on top of him; then, leaning forward, Johnny stretched his face toward Baldy's right arm, his mouth open and ready. Baldy was kicking Johnny's shins now and trying to keep his right arm from Johnny's gaping teeth. Then Johnny bit the arm, sinking his teeth into it until they hit the bone. Baldy screamed again; his fingers flew open and the knife slid to the floor. Johnny leaped to his feet and kicked the knife out of reach. Baldy too leaped up. Again they faced each other, but equal now. No! Johnny had miscalculated that broken pop bottle that he had dropped. There it was in

Baldy's right hand! Johnny went wild; he rushed at Baldy, heedless of the bottle, and rammed Baldy's head against the concrete wall. If Baldy wanted to kill him, then he would kill first. The bottle flew from Baldy's fingers and the bald head sagged limply. Johnny backed off, lifted his right fist and let it fly. Baldy staggered weakly over the dusty floor. Johnny followed, waiting for that bloody jaw to show itself at just the right angle. Baldy let down his guard a moment and Johnny caught him on the side of the head with a blow that sent hot pain flashing light-ninglike down the length of his arm. Baldy went down and lay still. Enraged, Johnny leaped upon Baldy, feeling that he had to blot out this beast once and for all.

79

"Naw, that's enough," Skinkie warned.

"I'll kill 'im," Johnny screamed.

"Naw, naw," Skinkie yelled. "That's enough. You won!" Skinkie grabbed Johnny and held him. "My God," Skinkie breathed. "You can fight."

Head down, Johnny stood in a corner, his chest heaving, his body so weak that he felt on the point of collapse, his eyes lingering balefully upon Baldy's prone form, staring at the bald head covered with blood and coal dust. Was Baldy dead? He hoped not.

He had not wanted to fight. He glanced at Skinkie, who was staring with amazement at the prostrate Baldy. Skinkie could now leap upon him and beat him, but he sensed that Skinkie's admiration for him ruled that out. Indeed, when Skinkie's eyes turned to him they were full of worshipful respect.

The door flew open and Treetop came rushing in. He stopped and gaped at Baldy's still body, then swept Skinkie's and Johnny's faces with a begging question.

"What in hell's happened?" Treetop demanded.

"This guy knocked Baldy cold," Skinkie related in tones of slow amazement.

"Is he dead?" Treetop asked in a whisper.

"Naw. Just out, cold," Skinkie said.

Johnny suddenly snapped out of his mood. Good God, he had to look after Baldy. He could not let the boy lie there and die, maybe . . . He bent slowly to the still form and gingerly touched the swollen jaw. No; it was not broken, just badly bruised and bleeding. But the right side of Baldy's jaw looked like a basketball, still swelling, the taut black skin glistening like a huge bubble.

"How did this happen?" Treetop asked disbelievingly.

"Never mind that," Johnny said. "You guys get

me some rags and cold water." He was assuming the role of leader man now, confidently, coolly.

Skinkie looked at Treetop and Treetop looked at Skinkie. Johnny rose and whirled upon them.

"Goddammit, get moving!" he shouted. "We can't let this fool lie here like this!" He felt Baldy's head. "He's getting fever . . ."

Meekly, obediently, Skinkie and Treetop got a can of water and a wad of rags. Johnny tenderly bathed Baldy's jaw and face. Baldy's eyelids flickered open and he groaned.

"How're you feeling?" Johnny asked him.

Baldy stared dully into Johnny's eyes, as though wondering if he were dreaming. He blinked and sighed:

"Goddamn, you beat me."

"You mad at me?" Johnny asked softly.

"Aw, hell no." He licked his battered lips. "You beat me."

"I didn't want to fight you," Johnny told him.

"You're a damned liar," Baldy said with baffled eyes.

"No. It's the truth," Johnny insisted. "I'm not afraid of you, but I didn't want to fight you."

"Then you're a crazy fool," Baldy stated flatly.

"Why?"

"'Cause if I could fight as well as you, I'd be fighting all the time," Baldy said.

"For what?"

"Hell, just to beat other people," Baldy said.

"I never fight unless I'm scared," Johnny said. "I've never been scared much, so I've never fought much," Johnny explained, still dabbing the wet rag over Baldy's jaw and cheek. "Baldy, you must be scared a lot to fight so much like—"

"You go to hell," Baldy said, but his voice was kind, resigned.

Johnny rose, pulled two desks together to form a kind of crude bed. He, with Treetop and Skinkie aiding him, lifted Baldy and stretched him out.

"OK, Bo," Baldy breathed, his eyes still baffled. Then he blurted: "Hell, if I'd beaten you like that I'd just kill you off. Why don't you just finish me off?"

"Why?" Johnny asked, blinking. "I don't want to kill anybody."

"OK, Bo," Baldy muttered, accepting what he did not understand.

Johnny realized that Baldy accepted no mercy and gave none, that he lived a life that was as hard on himself as it was on others, but Johnny could not realize how a boy could come to feel like that. Johnny looked steadily into Baldy's eyes but Baldy could only look at Johnny at intervals, and Johnny knew that he had beaten Baldy in more ways than one. Baldy was afraid of Johnny now, afraid that he knew more about life than he did, knew how to do things that were foreign to him. Baldy sighed and Johnny knew that he was surrendering more than his battered and bruised body, that he was giving up his role of leader man in the gang.

"OK," Baldy sighed again. "I was trying to kill you."

"You poor sonofabitch," Johnny muttered in pity.

Baldy smiled, lifted his head, brushed the wet rag aside and broke into a loud and long laugh. Skinkie and Treetop smiled, then joined in Baldy's laughter, laughing as though they had been released from a thralldom of fear. Johnny backed from them and looked on in disgust.

"You sure beat that bastard," Skinkie crooned in unstinted praise, his voice containing a new note. "Lord, you sure hit that bastard . . . he hit Baldy harder than I ever saw anybody hit." He broke into a hysterical laugh. "God, and that kick you gave 'im! Jesus, Baldy didn't fall. He just poured to the floor, like melted butter . . ."

83

"He really beat Baldy?" Treetop asked in a meek voice.

"Beat 'im? He mopped up the floor with 'im," Skinkie declared, lifting the fight to the level of legend. "I didn't even see your foot when you kicked his jaw. All I saw was your leg coming down. Baldy just stood there and the floor came up and met 'im. Ha, ha!" He shook his head, reveling in the memory of the blows and kicks. "Hope no sonofabitch ever kicks me like that. Say, Bo, did you ever play football?"

Johnny did not answer; he was savoring his triumph, wondering what he could do with it.

"You must've played football," Skinkie said, not minding Johnny's refusal to answer. "God, you could kill a man kicking him like that, kill 'im as dead as he'll ever die."

Baldy laughed and Johnny knew that Baldy was now thinking of the fight as though he had not been the victim, as though it had happened to someone else.

"I didn't know what the hell hit me," Baldy said, helping to establish the myth of his own defeat. "After that kick came, I couldn't believe that you'd done it. I was out on my feet." He wagged his head. "You're good all right." He paused and weighed

Johnny. "Well, we'll see how you do that again. You'll get plenty of chances . . ."

"What do you mean?" Johnny asked, uneasy.

"You'll see," Baldy said cryptically.

"You're just like a jackal," Treetop said.

"He is a jackal," Skinkie said, accepting the idea.

"Jackal . . . That's a good name," Baldy said, smiling dreamily.

"You have to be a jackal if you don't want to get killed," Johnny said, not quite understanding what was in their words.

"OK, Jackal," Treetop crooned.

"That's the way to fight," Baldy sang. "Fight with your hands and feet and teeth! If I ever fight Jackal again, I'm going to make 'im pull off his shoes. . . . Ha, ha!"

"They say that those Japs fight with their feet too," Treetop said.

"How's your jaw?" Johnny asked Baldy.

"It aches a little," Baldy admitted without shame.

"It'll feel better if you keep quiet," Johnny advised.

"Hell, this is nothing," Baldy said in a tone that made Johnny realize that he had been hurt many times.

"You oughn't've pulled that knife on me." Johnny sought for a way to atone for his kicking Baldy's jaw.

"That's old Baldy every time," Treetop intoned.

"He'll kill you if you make 'im mad," Skinkie seconded.

"But Baldy's not going to fight you anymore," Treetop assured Johnny.

"Naw, don't want to fight you anymore," Baldy said.

"You sure conquered that sonofabitch!" Skinkie shouted.

Baldy had fallen and now any old curse word was good enough to use on him. He no longer merited adulation; there was a new leader of the gang and, though they had not yet gone beyond the ceremony of naming him The Jackal, they were waiting for him to take over and lead them, to teach them his methods of self-defense, of outwitting their enemies, and of getting food and shelter. Treetop and Skinkie turned frankly now to Johnny.

"Jackal, you sure shot some pool tonight," Treetop said.

"He put Baldy's eight ball in the sidepocket," Skinkie said.

"He won the game," Baldy admitted. "And after he won it, he hit me over the head with the cue stick."

Johnny listened to the three of them guffaw. Baldy made an attempt to rise and fell senselessly back.

"He's out," Treetop said.

"He talked too much; he ought't've rested," Johnny said.

He placed his rolled coat beneath Baldy's slick head and felt for Baldy's pulse.

"He's all right," Skinkie jeered. "I've seen 'im worse than this."

Johnny stood studying Baldy's shining skull and the curiosity that had brought on the fight returned.

"Say," he asked of them, "how old is Baldy?"

"He's sixteen, but nobody'll believe it," Treetop told him.

Skinkie's and Treetop's laughter informed Johnny that Baldy was being repaid for all the terror and humiliation that he had inflicted upon his followers.

"It was his bald head that made 'im so mean," Skinkie revealed.

Baldy's eyes fluttered open, but his former supporters paid him no further attention, talking as if he were no longer there. And Baldy listened with calm resignation, with suffering, glazed eyes.

"But how did he get bald?" Johnny wanted to know.

"Well," Treetop drawled in enjoyment, "two years ago he caught a bad case of ringworm on his scalp at school. Everybody gets ringworm or lice at school once in a while, but Baldy had a terrific dose. And in his class a lot of white boys had it too. So the teacher sent them all to the principal, who called up the city hospital, and the hospital said send 'em right over. They sent a car for 'em, took 'em in grand style. . . ."

88

Johnny listened to Baldy, Treetop, and Skinkie laugh.

"And what happened?" Johnny prodded Treetop.

"Well, when those boys got to the hospital," Treetop resumed, "they put 'em all under X-ray machines to kill the ringworm. Pretty white nurses held their hands so that they wouldn't be scared . . ."

All four of them laughed now.

"Baldy had a head full of nice hair," Treetop related. "He was sitting under the X rays, just like the white boys, see? But those nurses were white and naturally they were paying more attention to the white boys than to Baldy. They forgot Baldy. All of a sudden Baldy felt an awful heat in his head. That X-ray machine was *frying* his brains!"

Prolonged and lazy laughter.

"Baldy yelled: 'Say, turn off that machine! My head's cooking!' A pretty white nurse ran and took a look, then clicked her tongue. 'Oh, doctor!' she called. 'Turn off the machine, *quick!* This nigger's too done . . . I see lard coming out of his head!'"

Baldy was so overcome with mirth that he groaned. Treetop beat his fists upon the top of the packing box and Skinkie stomped his feet as he pranced with joy in the candlelit room.

"And what happened then?" Johnny demanded eagerly.

"You can see what happened," Treetop said, pointing to Baldy's gleaming skull. "That X-ray machine killed every hair he had."

"What did Baldy do about it?" Johnny asked.

"What did he do?" Treetop asked ironically. "He told his folks at home and they laughed till they cried. His ma said: 'Serves you right. Now you've got something I didn't give you!'"

"What did you do then, Baldy?" Johnny pressed his questions.

"I spat in her face," Baldy said. "And left home."

89

Johnny sighed, recalling his own flight from home.

"Those white doctors got scared," Treetop continued. "They thought that Baldy was going to sue 'em about his hair, so they tried like hell to make it grow again. But that X-ray machine had done its work too well. Baldy came out of that hospital with his head as slick as grease, shining like a moon." Treetop howled. "He looked fifty years old. Folks used to stop 'im on the street and ask: 'Grandpa, can you tell me where Lenox Avenue is?' And when Baldy talked, his voice squeaky and piping like a baby sparrow's, the folks'd back off, scared." Treetop imitated how Baldy would answer: "'It's right over there, two blocks down . . .' And the folks'd run, thinking that they'd met a new kind of sissy!"

"You felt bad about it, didn't you, Baldy?" Johnny asked compassionately.

"Bad?" Treetop jeered. "Bad's no word for what he felt. He wouldn't go to school anymore after that. When he'd walk into the classroom, the boys and girls'd stand up and yell. Every time Baldy opened his mouth, there'd be a riot."

"They oughtn't've done that," Johnny mumbled, his eyes full of pain.

"Man, I couldn't help but laugh myself," Treetop

said. "He beat hell out of me for it, but I laughed till I cried."

"But why, Treetop?" Johnny asked, frowning.

"It was just funny," Treetop said. "One day Baldy got up and walked out of class and wouldn't go back. The truant officers looked for him, but Baldy always wore a cap."

"Was that the real reason why you quit school, Baldy?" Johnny asked.

"Yeah," Baldy confessed. "Folks wanted me to wear a wig, but wigs made my head sweat . . ."

"Then Billy found this place and we got this gang together," Skinkie said, patting Baldy affection- ately. "But Baldy, I never thought I'd see you stretched out like this . . . Ha, ha!"

"I'm OK," Baldy growled. "I can whip your ass anytime."

They laughed again, happy that Baldy's spirit was returning.

"If you so much as touch me, I'll sic The Jackal on you," Skinkie threatened.

Baldy managed to sit up, his eyes sober.

"I don't want to fight," Baldy intoned with sud- den firmness. "I'm quitting the gang."

Skinkie and Treetop were shocked. Johnny re- flected; if Baldy quit, the gang would break up; and if the gang broke up, where would he be? No, he could not let Baldy quit.

"Baldy, you can't quit," Johnny said.

"Well, The Jackal has the lead now," Skinkie said.

"Naw, you can't quit," Treetop chimed in.

"Why can't I quit?" Baldy demanded.

"For the same reason I can't quit," Johnny spoke harshly. "You might tell on us."

"That's telling 'im," Skinkie agreed.

"Did you hear 'im?" Treetop asked Baldy.

"You're in it as deep as we are," Skinkie reminded Baldy.

92

"The Jackal's our leader now," Treetop summed it up.

Silence. Johnny trembled. In assuming the role of the leader man of the gang, Johnny was both scared and glad: glad because at last he had crossed the frontier of childhood and had become a man, and scared because he feared failing his friends, scared because he did not feel hard and brutal enough. But what could he do? To have given up what he had so unintentionally won would have made the gang hate him enough to kill him. No; he had to pretend a courage that he did not feel and carry on, more for the sake of others than for his own.

"All right. Let's clean up this place," Johnny ordered.

They put the room to rights. All the while Johnny was wondering what Billy had told Treetop, but he did not want to ask.

"I'm still hungry," Skinkie said.

"Me too," Treetop said.

"Goddamn you, Baldy," Skinkie cursed. "If it hadn't been for you, we could've eaten our supper."

"Leave Baldy alone," Johnny scolded.

"OK, Jackal. What're we going to do?" Skinkie asked.

"What were you going to do before I came?" Johnny asked.

"We were going to Morningside Park and strong-arm somebody for some jack," Baldy spoke up. "Now we've got to do it, 'cause we're bone broke and hungry."

"I've never done anything like that," Johnny protested.

"Hell, it's nothing," Baldy said. "We'll show you."

Pride and fear fought in Johnny. Before him stood his awestruck followers, boys who were willing to accept his bare word as the living law of their lives.

"Are you scared, Jackal?" Treetop asked.

"Naw. I'm not scared a bit," Johnny lied. "I just don't know how to do it. You'll have to show me."

"It's easy," Baldy said. "We'll hide behind some bushes and wait for a white man to come along—one with some money, see? Then Treetop'll walk up to the man and ask 'im: 'Mister, give me a cigarette, please.' When that bastard reaches for his cigarettes, we grab 'im, put a hand over his mouth, an arm around his neck, a knee in his back, and throw 'im to the ground and strip 'im. The only thing is that you have to work fast." Baldy paused and studied Johnny. "You can do it. You're as quick as any man I've ever seen."

"All right," Johnny agreed. "But tell me just how you do it."

Baldy stood and began to reenact the projected robbery, and, in doing so, he was handing the sceptre of his leadership to Johnny.

"Treetop's got a good voice," Baldy outlined. "He's tall and people take him for being older than he is. He stops the white man and asks him for something. I leap out of the bushes, put a half Nelson on the white man's neck, squeezing the breath out of that bastard, then I bring my knee down into that bastard's back. He goes down like a stick of warm candy bending. While I'm doing that, Skinkie and Treetop and you will get on that white bastard like a million ants on a dead fly, see? He can't holler. I whisper to 'im: 'One peep, buddy, and you're a goner!' You, Skinkie, and Treetop'll go through his pockets. It's all over in less than a minute. The bigger they are, the quicker it is. You can't get a good hold on some of those little guys and they wriggle like hell; one even got away from me once. . . . Ready?"

"OK," Johnny nodded. "Let's go." He was nervous. If he did this, he would be forever cut off from the people he had known. But he had to eat.

"The main thing is time," Baldy explained. "If the bastard has no money on 'im, we take off his pants and run, see?"

"What time is it?" Johnny asked.

"It's after one," Skinkie said, studying his watch.

"Billy said you were solid," Treetop told Johnny at last.

Johnny sighed.

"All right, Jackal?" Baldy asked.

"Ready, Jackal?" Skinkie asked.

"We're all right behind you," Treetop pledged.

Johnny swallowed and his fingernails dug into his sweaty palms.

"All right! Let's go," Johnny sounded the tocsin for action, then led the way to the darkened streets, where a cold wind blew and a wan moon shone.

95

V

They kept their heads deep into their shoulders, assuming a stance that would obscure their features from passersby. Johnny watched his pals' movements and patterned his actions upon theirs, yearning to acquit himself well in the strange, dark world he had bargained to enter; yet deep in him a protest yelled against what he was doing. Had there been a way for him to have returned to his old home, he would have done so, but since he had to choose a new home, he wanted to make the choice himself.

He trailed Baldy, noticing that Treetop and Skinkie lingered to the rear. He heard Baldy's labored breathing and knew that the boy was still winded.

"Take it easy, Baldy," he said, draping his arm

about Baldy's shoulders.

"I'm OK," Baldy muttered.

"If you have fever, you'll catch pneumonia," Johnny cautioned.

"How do you know those things?" Baldy asked.

"Oh, everybody knows that," Johnny said lightly.

"Naw, they don't," Baldy said.

They reached a street intersection, keeping in the deep shadows cast by the buildings, averting their heads from solitary passersby.

"You're in our gang now," Baldy began in a low, serious tone. "So we've got to tell you everything."

"Sure," Johnny said.

"But if you spill it, it means your life," Baldy went on. "'Cause it'd mean the end of us. You see, we've figured this thing out to the last notch. Now, at night we use that room in the school basement, but in the day we've got another place. One of these days we're going to have a club all to ourselves. You're our new leader now and you've got to get busy on that."

"Where do we stay during the day?" Johnny asked.

"Over on a Hundred Thirty-third Street."

"In a room?"

"Naw. It's just a flat where we know a guy. He's a fence, see?"

"A fence?"

"Yeah. You know. The guy who sells the stuff we snatch." Baldy chuckled. "You'll learn. The flat's Gink's place. Gink's our fence, see? He gets rid of our stuff and gets us out of trouble."

"Uh-hunh," Johnny grunted.

"The one thing to remember in this game," Baldy revealed, "is the problem of hiding, to keep off the streets in the daylight hours. I'm only on the street half an hour a day. Don't let folks learn your face."

"I see," Johnny said.

"We've done this a year and nobody has pointed a finger at us yet," Baldy went on. "We're safe as long as we keep our mouths shut and don't show off. This is a job like any other. Do it right, and you get paid well. But if you start ratting on the job, the boss'll get you—"

"The boss?" Johnny asked. "You mean Gink?"

"Naw. Ha, ha! I mean the cops," Baldy said.

"Why do you call the cops our boss?" Johnny asked, feeling his view of the world being violently wrenched.

"The cops are really our boss," Baldy informed

him. "Gink sells the stuff we snatch to a Jewish contact and pays off the cops. Cross the cops, and you're finished. Now, we—"

Baldy's voice broke off and Johnny looked at him. Baldy was peering ahead into the night.

"A cop," Baldy whispered. "You always got to look out for 'em."

Johnny waited for Baldy to give the signal. Baldy whirled to Treetop and Skinkie.

"Scatter," Baldy whispered fiercely. "We meet at the park's entrance."

The boys vanished like ghosts, melting into the night's blackness.

99

"Follow me," Baldy said, darting arrowlike off to the right.

Johnny sped behind Baldy, noticing that Baldy ran without making a sound; he imitated Baldy, lifting his weight on his toes, reducing the noise of his shoes.

"You'll have to wear tennis shoes," Baldy panted as they slowed. "OK, we can stop now." Baldy chuckled. "Ha, ha! That cop knew us."

"Then why did we run?" Johnny asked.

"'Cause if he sees us, he might think he's being watched and he'll pinch us," Baldy explained.

They passed houses whose windows loomed black and silent. Now and then a man or a woman passed, but Baldy did not glance at them.

"It's about time for some white sucker to show up," Baldy commented. "Man, these white folks sure think some funny things about us in Harlem. White men are always poking around us, trying to find a colored gal, especially those white soldier boys. They hate us, but they like our women." Baldy's voice grew menacing. "One night a nice-looking white boy, a little drunk, came up to me and asked: 'Shine, where can I get some black meat?' He didn't even notice my face when he said 'shine.' He must've thought all colored folks were crazy. I wanted to kill 'im right then and there, but I waited. 'You want a gal?' I asked him. 'Yeah, and some whiskey,' he said. I said: 'Yeah, I know where you can get just what you want.' I led that bastard to a stoop, opened a door, and said: 'Just stand here and wait.' He says, 'OK.' He was grinning. How come white folks trust us so when they know damn well what they've done to us? If I was white, I'd never trust a nigger sonofabitch. . . . He stood there, waiting, thinking about a hot black gal. I took out my knife, pressed the button. Man, when I stuck that blade right through his navel, he said: 'Ur-rrrhmp!' and slid to the floor."

"You stabbed 'im?"

"I read in the papers that I killed 'im," Baldy recited unemotionally. "But I didn't stay there to see 'im die. I took a hundred sixty from that buzzard's pockets."

Johnny felt cold. He walked on, wrapped in a sense of nightmare. The night wind was icy on his forehead, but when he rubbed it he found sweat there.

"What happened?"

"Nothing. They found 'im and gave 'im a military funeral, I reckon," Baldy said.

"I don't like killing," Johnny said.

"Oh, now, Jackal, don't get me wrong," Baldy protested heatedly. Then he laughed. "I don't brag about killing. But, hell, you've got to kill somebody sometime or other. Somebody's always going to get killed. It's all just a matter of time. The correct thing to do is to make sure it's the other man."

"Have you killed many people?" Johnny asked through clenched teeth.

"Now, look, don't you go making me out worse than I am," Baldy scolded with deep moral fervor. "If you stay in this racket, you'll find out what you've got to do."

Johnny wanted to flee to the shelter of one of

those dark looming houses and knock on the door and be admitted into the warmth of a home where people lived with smiles and trust and faith; he yearned to sink to his knees to some kind old black woman and sob: "Help me . . . I can't go through with this!" But he could not do that; they would call the police and have him sent to jail. He was even a fool to think of finding a home again. There was nobody he could run to. He had to stay with Baldy and Treetop and Skinkie.

"On your toes," Baldy whispered. "Keep your eyes skinned. We're almost there."

Treetop and Skinkie were coming, one behind the other, keeping close to the buildings. The streets were empty and silent, with streetlamps burning like yellow torches. The moon hung over the edge of a roof-broken horizon. Then the pavement vibrated from the thundering rush of an underground train.

"A train's stopping," Baldy said. "Let's go into the park and lay for somebody."

Johnny followed Baldy, who sped like a jungle cat up a dirt path, then crouched at Baldy's side beside a granite ledge bordering a sloping lawn. They were screened by a bush and from the height of the ledge Johnny could see the dark path spreading before him.

"We wait here," Baldy said.

"You there, Jackal?" Treetop whispered.

"I'm in all the way," Johnny swore.

Baldy climbed atop the ledge and lay flat. Treetop now took his place boldly in the dirt pathway, striding to and fro. Skinkie knelt behind a bush. Overhead were the moon and a few lonely stars. Taut, Johnny fastened upon each detail, for he wanted to remember how these things went, yet, cutting sharply across his high-pitched resolve, was a dim, echoing memory of home. From where he waited by the ledge he could hear the city breathing quietly, like an animal about to spring. Then he was startled to hear Baldy speak aloud:

"No suckers this trip. We'll just wait."

"Oh, somebody'll come," Skinkie said.

"I hope they're loaded with dough," Treetop called.

"How do you know how to pick 'em?" Johnny asked.

"That's easy," Baldy said. "You can always tell. . . . Last week we jumped a university teacher . . ."

"A man who teaches in that school on the hill?" Johnny asked.

"Yeah, man," Baldy chuckled. "We read in the

papers afterwards that he was a whiz in mathematics, that he could figure out how far it was to the moon. When I had that bugger on the ground, he yelled: "Don't hurt me, boys! You think I'm against your people, but you're wrong . . . I love your race!'" Baldy guffawed. "That bastard knew that so many of his kind had done things to us that as soon as I grabbed 'im, he wanted to yell: 'It wasn't me who killed your ma! . . .'"

The boys laughed softly in the moonlight, still waiting.

"Did you ever jump a black man?" Johnny asked.

"Yes. White or black; they're all the same," Baldy said.

"But I'd rather jump a white man," Treetop said.

"Yeah. Somehow it feels better," Skinkie said.

"Sh!" Treetop signaled.

Silence. Johnny strained his ears. Somebody was coming briskly forward. Would Treetop jump this one? Were cops nearby? Would they be caught? Johnny waited, hearing the footsteps coming nearer, the tips of his fingers gripping the granite ledge. He saw Baldy tensing on top of the ledge. Then there followed silence in which the *pack-pack-pack* of approaching footsteps came nearer and nearer. The footsteps seemed to be going past now. Had Treetop decided not to attack the man? What was happening? *Pack-pack-pack* . . . The footsteps went past.

"What was the matter, Treetop?" Baldy asked.

"Some goddamn zoot-suiter," Treetop sneered. "If it'd rain on that coat he's wearing, it'd draw up and choke 'im to death!"

There was loud laughter that died away.

"Sh!" Treetop cautioned.

Johnny saw a white man heaving into view. *Pack-pack-pack* . . . He was tall, well-dressed, and carried a walking stick. Instinct told him that this man would be their victim. *Pack-pack-pack* . . . Then he could hear the footsteps no more. Treetop's voice came smooth and innocent:

105

"Pardon me, Mister . . . But how do I get to One Hundred Twenty-fifth Street? I'm a stranger here. I got lost."

Johnny marveled at how well Treetop was doing his job. Then he heard the white man's voice:

"Oh, ha, ha . . . For a moment, boy, I thought you were one of those muggers. Good to see a well-behaved colored boy for a change. Well, keep walking down this path and soon you'll come to Morningside Avenue. Then turn to your right. By the way, have you a home here?"

There came the sound of a rough scraping of feet,

RICHARD   WRIGHT

then a loud grunt. Johnny looked for Baldy and
Skinkie, but they had already sprinted away. Things
were happening too fast for him. He rushed out into
the open and was amazed to see that the white man
had been pinned flat upon his back, his head crooked
in Baldy's arm. White and helpless, the white man's
face was tilted to the sky, mouth gaping, white teeth
showing. Skinkie and Treetop were rifling the man's
pockets, pulling out papers, a handkerchief . . . Not a
word was spoken. Long gasping sounds of the man's
breathing . . . Johnny went closer. Treetop sprang up,
muttering:

106

"I got it!"

"Strip 'im; he's tough," Baldy ordered tensely.

What followed was so rapid that Johnny's eyes
could scarcely follow it; Treetop loosened the man's
belt and Skinkie jerked off the man's trousers, which
was to prevent the man's running to give alarm, to
intimidate him with partial nakedness.

"Take his goddamn shoes!" Baldy ordered.

Treetop now jerked off the man's shoes.

"I'm loosening my arm on you, sucker," Baldy
hissed. "But don't move!"

"Awright, awright . . . Take my money, boys, but
don't hurt me . . ."

"Shut up!" Baldy said, waving a knife blade at the

man. He gave a low whistle. Like robots, Treetop and Skinkie, with Johnny following, raced off behind a fleeing Baldy, their feet skimming over greensward. Running, Johnny turned his head to look at the white man and he was startled to see the man standing beside a woman! *What was that?* Then he heard a yell:

"YOU BOYS!"

Had someone seen them? The image of the man and the woman standing beside him stuck in his mind: two forms outlined clearly in the moonlight. The woman's screams came sharply now:

"YOU BOYS! YOU BOYS!"

Yes, it was a Negro woman . . . Johnny had seen her in a moment's turning of his head and he wanted to tell his pals that a woman had seen the mugging, and that she was screaming. Baldy, Skinkie, and Treetop were far ahead of him. Ought he yell for Baldy to stop? No, they'd think that he was scared. Still he heard the woman's faint screams:

"YOU BOYS! YOU BOYS!"

And he was sure that his pals had not heard her. They neared a street and Baldy called:

"Stop, now."

They huddled together, panting. Johnny wondered if he ought to tell them about that screaming woman, that maybe she'd seen them. No. But the woman seemed to have been running after them, advancing towards them over the park.

"Put those shoes and pants under your coat," Baldy ordered Treetop.

"Right," Treetop said.

"You got the wallet?" Skinkie asked.

"Hell, yes," Treetop said.

"How was it?" Baldy asked, grinning at Johnny.

Johnny hesitated a moment, then said:

"Good, neat, fast."

"Think you can do it now?" Treetop asked.

"Sure. There's nothing to it," Johnny said.

Again Johnny wondered if he ought to tell them about the woman; he turned his head and looked over the park, but no one was in sight. Had he imagined that he had seen and heard the woman? No, he had seen her, had heard her. He found himself identifying himself with the woman, pictured her running and looking for them, and he wanted her to find them.

"What's the matter, Jackal?" Baldy asked. "You see somebody?"

"Naw. Just keeping my eyes peeled," Johnny mumbled.

"You're all right. Sharp."

"Where to now?" Johnny asked.

"Gink's," Baldy said. He turned to Johnny. "Suppose we met a cop now? What'd you do?"

"We'd split up," Johnny said slowly, still hearing the yelling woman, still seeing her in his mind.

"Then what would you do?" Baldy pressed him.

"I'd duck into a vestibule," Johnny said, still aching to tell of the woman he had glimpsed.

"That's not good enough," Baldy corrected him kindly. "When you go into that vestibule, keep right on up to the roof, see? Then cross over to other buildings. You'll come across a fire escape and then you can come down."

"I see," Johnny said, hugging his knowledge of the woman secretly and fiercely to his heart.

With Johnny and Baldy leading and Treetop and Skinkie following some twenty-five yards to the rear, they walked eight blocks to Gink's place. But Johnny's mind was still full of the running and invisible woman that he had seen and heard. Now and then he could not help but turn his head.

"What're you worried about?" Baldy asked him.

"Nothing," Johnny mumbled peevishly.

"Treetop and Skinkie can take care of themselves," Baldy said. "Don't be nervous."

They halted in front of a tall brownstone building.

VI

Johnny filed in behind Baldy; then he was running up the stairs, hearing Treetop and Skinkie following. But he was wishing that the woman he had seen were trailing them. But why did he feel like that? Was he already disloyal? No, he did not wish to get caught. But did he? They halted on a rickety landing on the fifth floor and Baldy rapped three times, then once. Footsteps sounded; a metal bolt clinked; a chain rattled; and the door opened slowly.

A tall, skinny black man confronted them; his neck seemed like a dry black stick, but his head was huge and his eyes were large and bulging and watery. At first sight Johnny did not like him and once again the image of the running and yelling woman in the park hovered compulsively in his mind. But if he told about her now, they would ask why he had not spoken before. Looking at Gink's face, he wanted that strange woman to come and find him. . . .

"Let us in," Baldy said.

The lips of Gink's small mouth hung open all the time, showing stained, wide-apart teeth, reminding Johnny of a quiet, waiting rat.

"Come in," Gink spoke softly, rapidly. "It's cold in this hall."

"Come on, Jackal," Baldy gestured.

"Whoa," Gink balked, spreading his arms. "Who's this?"

"I'll tell you all about 'im," Baldy said. "Let us in."

Johnny had a wild wish that Gink would not admit him, would drive him out into the cold dark streets where he could find the woman who had yelled after them.

"OK," Gink mumbled, eyeing Johnny closely. "You didn't tell me you had anybody new."

"He's OK," Baldy said.

"What does he do?" Gink demanded.

"He's a Moocher, like us," Baldy explained.

Gink's eyes smiled, but his lips did not move.

111

"So you skipped a foster home too, hunh?" Gink asked Johnny.

"Yeah," Johnny said.

Skinkie and Treetop entered and stood while Baldy and Gink discussed Johnny.

"He's leader man from now," Baldy said. "He's terrific."

"A killer if I ever saw one," Treetop underscored Baldy's words.

"We call 'im Jackal," Skinkie said.

"Where'd you find 'im," Gink asked.

"Billy sent 'im," Baldy said.

"Oh. All right," Gink said, closing and bolting the door. "How did you make out, tonight?"

Treetop handed over the wallet, a watch, and a stickpin.

"We didn't touch the wallet," Baldy said. "We don't know what's in it."

"I'll tell you in a minute," Gink said, going to a table and emptying the wallet.

Johnny looked uneasily around; the room resembled a department store—there were piles of shirts, cameras, radios, typewriters . . . Gink saw Johnny's wide eyes and he chuckled.

"Never saw so much stuff, hunh?" Gink asked.

"Naw," Johnny sighed, still seeing and hearing that running woman in the park.

"Good haul tonight," Gink said, holding up a batch of green bills. He fingered the watch and stick-pin. "I'll make it a round fifty dollars apiece. All right?"

"OK," Baldy said. "Next time you deal with Jackal, see?"

"Fifty dollars all right for tonight, Jackal?" Gink asked.

"OK," Johnny said.

Gink counted bills into each extended palm.

113

"Well, Jackal, how do you feel?" Gink asked as he placed a wad of notes into Johnny's hand.

"Fine. Nice place you got here," Johnny mumbled.

"He sounds like a schoolteacher," Gink said and they all laughed. "Listen, a big haul like this might bring cops out. You boys better keep under cover tonight."

"Right," Baldy said.

"Bunk in the back room if you're sleepy," Gink suggested.

"I'm beat," Baldy said.

Gink led them down a hallway heaped with

merchandise, then pointed to a row of cots in a back room.

"Anybody hungry?" Gink asked.

"I'm starved," Treetop cried.

"What've you got to eat, Gink?" Skinkie asked.

"Salami, beer, and bread," Gink said. "Help yourself out of the icebox."

Baldy spread the food upon a newspaper upon the floor and all but Johnny squatted around it.

"Why won't you eat, Jackal?" Baldy asked.

"Not hungry," Johnny said, feeling his stomach muscles too tight to eat a mouthful.

"You did all right. Don't be nervous," Skinkie said.

"I'm not nervous," Johnny said.

Johnny sat brooding while the others ate and chatted. Gink hovered, watching Johnny.

"Why don't you lie down," Gink prompted Johnny.

"Thanks. I guess I will," he said, stretching out upon a cot.

Later the light was dimmed and they rested. One by one they fell asleep, but Johnny remained awake, staring into the shadows. Soon he heard the others' snoring and he felt better. He could think of that running and yelling woman in the park now without feeling too guilty. Oh, if she could only find him! Once or twice, as he was about to doze, Johnny heard Gink's soft footsteps padding through the room. Where was he? How had he come here? But it was foolish to even ask himself such questions; he had made his choice, the only choice that had lain within his reach. He sighed and turned over on his back, looking at the dingy ceiling. Fatigue sapped his bones. He felt his eyelids drooping. But he forced himself, for a reason he did not know, to remain awake. Then he was once more drifting toward sleep, seeing that running and yelling woman, hearing:

115

"YOU BOYS! YOU BOYS!"

Finally Johnny was dreaming, dreaming that the woman had come and had found him, and yet, while dreaming, knowing full well that she would never come, that he was alone, knowing that no such voice would call him home, reprove him with love, chastise him with devotion, or place a cool soft hand upon his brow when he was fevered with doubt and indecision; knowing that he was alone and had to go on alone to make a life for himself by trying to reassemble the shattered fragments of his lonely heart.

AFTERWORD

lthough *Rite of Passage* is being published for the first time more than thirty years after Richard Wright's death, it is unmistakably a story from the heart of Wright's consciousness and creativity. Indeed, for those familiar with even a part of his body of fiction—his novels, novellas, and short stories—it is not difficult to guess at once that this story was written by Richard Wright and almost certainly by no one else. Within these pages may be found many of the character types, themes, situations, metaphors, and images that distinguish Wright from other major writers. However, this is not to say that *Rite of Passage* is predictable. Far from it. Here Wright takes raw material dear to him and adapts it in such a fashion that we have yet another angle into his remarkable sensibility and soul.

The publication of *Rite of Passage* now is opportune, for Wright was far ahead of his time in several ways but above all in illuminating the relationships among racism, juvenile delinquency, violent crime, and the black urban ghettos of America. Within the last ten years, Manhattan, the setting of *Rite of Passage*, has witnessed at least two highly publicized tragedies that might have been anticipated and imagined by Wright as seen in his various works, including *Rite of Passage*. The first was the shooting of a black youth, a resident of Harlem attending one of the most exclusive preparatory schools in America, by a white undercover policeman, who accused the youth and his brother of attempting to mug him—in the same general area, Morningside Heights, in which Wright sets the mugging that brings the action of *Rite of Passage* to a climax. The second tragedy was the sadly notorious "Central Park jogger" episode of 1989, in which a group of black youths, also teenagers, attacked and beat a young white woman running alone at night in the park. Although many people were shocked by both episodes, Wright clearly was able, fifty years before, when this novella was

first begun, to see events of a similar tragedy and in-
humanity coming because of social conditions that
were producing unprecedented levels of alienation
and rage in the young.

Fifteen-year-old Johnny Gibbs easily takes his
place among the ranks of the protagonists in Wright's
fiction. He takes his place in the broad but nevertheless relatively uniform band represented, on the one
hand, by Bigger Thomas, the desperate hero of *Native
Son* (1940), and, on the other, Cross Damon of *The
Outsider* (1953), the most intellectual and literate of
all of Wright's heroes. (It must be stressed that despite his intelligence, Cross is as misguided in his
own way and is at least as murderous as Bigger
Thomas.) Because of his youth, Johnny more readily
resembles characters such as Big Boy, of Wright's remarkable story "Big Boy Leaves Home," which was
published in *Uncle Tom's Children* (1938); or the hero
of "Almos' a Man," the boy who shoots a mule by
mistake, in Wright's *Eight Men* (1961). Nevertheless,
Johnny, as an excellent student in a Northern urban
setting, is probably most like Cross Damon of *The
Outsider*, if we can imagine Cross at this early stage of
his life. If Johnny is indeed an anticipation of Cross,
then his fate might be quite complex. Cross's intelli-

gence and literacy lead him to a sense of himself as Godlike, with God's power to create life and also to take it.

In keeping with several of Wright's black heroes, Johnny is jolted out of his innocence into the stark realization of the world as a hostile place. In perhaps Wright's most dramatic and memorable depiction of a black boy's sudden loss of innocence, "Big Boy Leaves Home," the hero and his young friends lose their innocence when they unwittingly transgress the central taboo of the white South, that which prohibits even the thought or appearance of a personal relationship between a black man (or a grown boy) and a white woman. In *Rite of Passage*, Johnny does not collide with a racial taboo. Instead, his life is changed by the government bureaucracy in the area of human welfare and social services—although the way this bureaucracy (which may include some blacks) treats young blacks must have much to do with race and racism. The power and carelessness of the white world may be inferred from the policies and actions of the authorities who insist that Johnny must be sent to a new home, even as it is clear that these authorities have only the most limited respect for blacks and the poor in general. "Son, you see," he is told by his foster mother, "the City folks came and told me that you had to leave us. They didn't say why. You didn't do anything wrong; nobody's mad at you. It seems that after a child's been in a foster home for a certain number of years, they move 'im to another home. I begged 'em, prayed to 'em, but they said that was the rule."

As in virtually all of Wright's work, race and racism are potent factors in *Rite of Passage*. The power of whites to affect the lives of blacks is clear and ever present. Wright refers to isolated examples of racism, or of careless attitudes of whites toward blacks, such as the negligence that leads to the gang member Baldy losing his hair and acquiring his nickname, as well as much of his bitterness and malevolence. Authority is generally white and alien to the lives of these Harlem blacks. Johnny's teacher, a white woman, is seen as a responsible, caring professional, but Johnny believes that he cannot turn to her for help outside of school. The police, most of whom presumably are white, do their job but are also depicted as corrupt; on the take, they are ready both to punish transgressors and to profit from street crime.

Race probably shows itself most tellingly in a subtle way: The black world of Johnny and his family seems powerless and inept, without any sustained, complex institutions that can translate into the ameliorative power of civilization. As in so much of Wright's fiction, blacks exist in a *culture* (as do blacks and whites alike in the South); civilization and its glories are beyond their reach. Wright's idea here is that civilization is not a natural quality (as culture is) but one that must be fostered over the generations and centuries by traditions of learning and teaching that are possible only among free people who respect one another. Here he does not emphasize the dehumanizing effects of slavery and Jim Crow that he stresses in his autobiography *Black Boy* (1945), but the sense of African-American culture in Harlem is still almost palpable as a thin, dingy, deprived, and marginal culture. The surest indication of that thinness and marginality is the fact that when young blacks like Johnny or Baldy cannot function within their culture and the world in general, they fall fast and hard into crime, violence, and despair. No safety net exists for such people.

One ominous result is the fear and hatred blacks feel toward whites. For many readers this fear and hatred, but especially the hatred, had been the historic revelation of *Native Son*. The victim of the mugging, chosen at random by the gang of boys, is white, as are most of the victims of the gang. Whites are undoubtedly chosen because they are likely to have more money than blacks, but the element of revenge is also present. Baldy almost delights in telling of killing a white man, and by reflex he identifies prospective mugging victims as white. Skinkie and Treetop would both prefer to mug whites. "Yeah," Skinkie says. "Somehow it feels better."

Rite of Passage also reflects many of Wright's ideas about the general dynamics of antisocial behavior, especially those within the African American community. One of these ideas is about the predominance of fear in the culture—in general, as a response to racism and segregation, but also in the context of criminal behavior. An example of the former is the timid response of adults to the city bureaucrats; examples of the latter may be found in abundance among Baldy and his gang, including boys like Treetop and Skinkie, who are intimidated by Baldy and live in "a thralldom of fear." After Baldy is defeated by Johnny, they are released from this "thralldom" but enter into another, this time to Johnny. A measure of Johnny's superiority as a human being is his relative fearlessness in general, and his intelligent recognition of the place of fear in violence. "I never fight unless I'm scared," he admits; then he tells the vicious Baldy: "Baldy, you must be scared a lot to fight so much."

Another measure is the power of his alienation. In this story, Wright carefully establishes the moment when Johnny is first dominated by the idea of his estrangement and alienation. "The feeling of estrangement that had set in," the narrative declares, "when his mother and sister had told him that he was going to go to a new home now draped him like a black cowl; it was a feeling that was to remain with him all his life, a feeling out of which he was to act and live, a feeling that would stay with him so long that he would eventually forget that it was in him." The age of fifteen is probably rather late for so dramatic a change in an individual's psychology. Although it is certainly possible to initiate in one's teen years a life-long sense of alienation, this moment in Johnny's life is probably best seen as a token, in some respects, of Wright's interest in individuals who are virtually born alienated, a position with which he seemed to identify personally. What is made clear is that, in the end, Johnny defines himself by his sense of aloneness, of "knowing that he was alone and had to go on alone to make a life for himself by trying to reassemble the shattered fragments of his lonely heart."

In *Rite of Passage*, as in most of Wright's fiction, young black men receive little or no aid or guidance, much less love and attention, from adult black males. When Johnny learns the truth about his past, he discovers that even his real mother does not know who his father is. Mr. Gibbs, his foster father, is absent during the story (he is at work) and appears to have no controlling influence over Johnny after fifteen years of living together. "I've got a father," Johnny protests, when he is told he must leave and go to a new home. "Pa's my father." But Mr. Gibbs's authority and influence seem to amount to nothing in stopping Johnny from running away.

Instead, women dominate Johnny's life—his teacher, his foster mother, Big Sis, and the shadowy, screaming woman at the end of the story. Again, this is a typical feature of Wright's fiction. Personifying the cruelty of some women to their children is Baldy's mother, who mocks him after he loses his hair. "Serves you right," she tells him. "Now you've got something I didn't give you!" Baldy's response is also vicious. "I spat in her face," he tells Johnny. "And left home." More typically in Wright, however, women are not so aggressive. In *Rite of Passage*, as in other works, the foster mother of the central character, Johnny, is defined by a quality of helplessness that deeply affects the boy and compromises his love for her. Johnny's real mother is also a victim. She conceived him one night after drinking too much; then, abandoned by his father, she descended into madness and an insane asylum. Almost certainly Wright was influenced, in these depictions, by his relationship with his own mother. Her abandonment by her own husband (Richard's father) and her chronic illness, including partial paralysis, throughout his boyhood and beyond left him with a sense of her as passive, suffering, and depressed, and as a handicap to him in his struggle to become a man and make something of himself beyond what the South prescribed. (However, Wright loved and never abandoned his mother, but instead supported her for the rest of her life.)

Nevertheless, perhaps the most memorable woman in the story for both Johnny and the reader is of a different kind altogether. She is the unnamed woman, most likely a fiction of Johnny's conscience and imagination, who attempts to make the gang members face up to the moral outrage of their actions in mugging an innocent man. She represents more than moral outrage: She stands for love, decency, and the comforts of home—or for Johnny's desire for all of these factors. Even before the mugging, as he sees the terrible deed he is being drawn into, Johnny thinks of a woman, and about the virtues she represents: "He yearned to sink to his knees to some kind old black woman and sob: 'Help me . . . I can't go through with this!'" Looking back as he flees after the crime, Johnny sees the man standing next to a woman, who screams at them only two words: "YOU BOYS! YOU BOYS!" Responding immediately and instinctively to her meaning, Johnny even imagines the woman running after them, chasing them. Thinking of her as "running and invisible," he hugs "his knowledge of the woman secretly and fiercely to his heart." Even after his sense of guilt about the mugging begins to abate, he continues to hear her. "Oh," Johnny yearns, "if she could only find him!"

127

Atypical of most of the rest of Wright's work, *Rite of Passage* presents a black woman standing for the finest human qualities, those qualities that make a difference between suffering and despair, on the one hand, and happiness and hope, on the other. She is "home." When he loses her, Johnny knows that "no such voice would call him home, reprove him with love, chastise him with devotion, or place a cool soft hand upon his brow when he was fevered with doubt and indecision." This tribute is possible because theirs is essentially a maternal relationship. The fact that Johnny and his friends are boys, rather than men, allows Wright to envision a woman as a symbol of human nurturing. If Johnny is ever going to be helped by a mature woman, in an adult love relationship, to grow out of his sense of alienation, we are given no indication of such a future in this story. The bond between mother and son has been cut, and with that severance, other ties of love between that son and other women are difficult, if not impossible.

Wright's main way of underscoring this bleak view of the possibility of love is by his deployment of situations and images of violence. In this way, *Rite of Passage* is of a piece with the rest of his fiction. Few major American writers are more fascinated in their art by depictions of violence, especially acts of violence in which the head is brutalized, than he was. Perhaps the most infamous example of this violence in Wright concerns Mary Dalton, who in *Native Son* is accidentally smothered, then is decapitated and has her body burned; also in that novel, Bigger kills his girlfriend Bessie by smashing her head repeatedly with a brick, then throwing her body down an air shaft. In *Rite of Passage*, Baldy, who carries a gun, boasts of having once stabbed a white sailor to death. The fight between Johnny and Baldy for the leadership of the gang is perhaps the single most protracted violent struggle in all of Wright, with a knife and a broken bottle and a savage kick to the head: "The shoe met Baldy's chin bone, sounding like rifle shot, sending Baldy's head back as though some steel wire had jerked it. Baldy slid to the floor, limp, groaning in semiconsciousness, his lips slobbering foam and blood."

129

In the gang of boys—Baldy, Skinkie, Treetop, and Johnny—Wright creates an almost surreal and macabre representation of ghetto youth who have lost hope. It is worth noting how Wright's vision of urban black culture had become more sour with the passing years. The foursome is a refiguring of black manhood as first represented in Wright's fiction by the four men at the center of his first novel, the posthumously published *Lawd Today!* (1963). In that novel, the men, who are friends and postal workers in Chicago, epitomize the waste of human energy in idleness, lechery, gambling, and superstition. However, compared to these men, who at least love the basic pleasures of life and are full of laughter, the boys in *Rite of Passage* are far more forbidding. Skinkie's "bloodshot eyes hinted at cruelty and a mysterious reserve of brute strength." Treetop is tall, thin, and muddy-colored; his face is covered with pimples, "many of which ran with watery matter." His face exuded "a terrible intensity." Baldy, "squat, black, thick," is sixteen but looks like fifty, according to the text. With his ancient look but squeaking adolescent's voice, he terrifies strangers, who see him as a mutant. A walking death's head, or skull, he represents the absolute demise of the human spirit. Thus Wright seems to prefigure the lives of young black men who cannot make it in the city; we see no other rival or parallel lives to counter this picture of horror.

Rite of Passage is vintage Wright in other respects. It takes place not simply in the city but in the tenements that produced Bigger Thomas. Going home at the start of the story, Johnny sees "the garishly painted yellow walls of the corridor" of his apartment. "He had lived in this smelly, ramshackle tenement all his life," the text notes. Although a college (City College of the City of New York, or CCNY) sits on a hill in the neighborhood, it has little to do with the daily lives of the people who live there. The city here is seen not as a place of avenues and elegant buildings but in virtual darkness, at night, in seedy tenements and basement rooms. A park is a feature of this cityscape, but Morningside Park—in this story—is not for citizens to enjoy trees and flowers but a jungle where muggers attack and rob people almost with impunity.

Begun by Wright in the spring of 1945, and first called "The Jackal," *Rite of Passage* was conceived in the immense shadow cast by Wright's autobiography *Black Boy*, which appeared that same year. The first pages of *Rite of Passage* were written even as Wright waited nervously for the public reaction to a book unlike any previously seen in African American or American autobiography. *Black Boy* tells in graphic detail about Wright's boyhood and adolescence in Mississippi, Arkansas, and Memphis, Tennessee, and his departure from the South as a youth of seventeen for the North in search of freedom and a new life. The autobiography is a young man's tale of cruel rejection by his father, the lingering paralytic illness of his mother, the repressive censure of other family members, the lack of sympathy and understanding he encountered from the rest of the black community, and the outright hatred and racism of the white South.

The hero, Richard Wright, leaves for the North determined to try to make something of his life in spite of these destructive forces that have sought—in his telling—to do nothing less than break his morale, impoverish his spirit and sense of self, and ruin his creative powers as an artist.

As broad and deep as were Wright's intellectual and social concerns as he made his way in the world and matured as a thinker and writer, he remained crucially interested in the lives and fates of young people, and especially the lives and fates of young black men. As a Communist, he had been drilled in the lesson of the importance of the social implications of literature, but it seems clear that his own independent sense of that connection went beyond ideology. Intellectually and emotionally at some distance from the black communities in which he lived, whether in the South, on the South Side of Chicago, or in Harlem in New York, he nevertheless remained profoundly interested in what happened to his fellow African Americans there. He sought to be an objective intellectual, but he had a deep concern for the culture of black Americans, and especially—by this time—the culture of the young men among the black migrants settled in the cities of the North. (Wright had moved to New York from Chicago in 1937, and was still living there when he started *Rite of Passage*.)

Wright was acutely aware of the psychological stresses, as well as economic and political stresses, that marked the daily lives of these people. For this reason, and despite the common prejudices against psychiatry and the stigma attached to virtually any admission of mental instability, he willingly joined in an effort, about the same time as he began writing *Rite of Passage*, by the psychiatrist Dr. Louis Wertham to found the first psychiatric clinic in Harlem. Thus, too, Wright became interested also about the same time in the work of the Wiltwyck School for Boys. Located in a beautiful, rural setting in the foothills of the Catskill Mountains, in Esopus, New York, Wiltwyck boldly acknowledged these psychological stresses, and sought to apply the latest theories and practices of psychiatric social work to the rehabilitation of the young delinquents it aimed to help and change.

The Wiltwyck School is directly in the background of the story *Rite of Passage*. Housing some eighty troubled boys, who were supervised by a staff of about twenty professionals (this extraordinary ratio was intended to ensure that each boy finally received the attention he presumably had always lacked), Wiltwyck was founded in direct response to a growing crisis of juvenile delinquency among blacks in New York. Wright himself noted perhaps the most daunting statistic about juvenile delinquency in Manhattan (that is, Harlem) at this time. Of the 1.7 million people in Manhattan, only 300,000 were African American; yet blacks accounted for 53 percent of all juvenile delinquents in the borough.

Wright believed that he knew exactly why this discrepancy existed, why so many young blacks were falling into a life of crime and so many black families were falling apart. One hardly needs to go beyond his autobiography, *Black Boy*, for an explanation, or for illustrations of how the white South systematically and ruthlessly crushed the souls of blacks and kept them from acquiring those qualities that would lift individuals out of life in a culture and into the arms of true civilization. The North was less openly hostile and repressive, but still no haven for migrant blacks and their children, who were shunted into special neighborhoods and denied almost all jobs except where they were absolutely needed. In Manhattan, black Harlem had enjoyed a mild vogue at one point in the 1920s, but the riots there in 1935 and in 1943 showed that behind the façade of joy and dance and song was the stark reality of poverty, disillusionment, and despair.

Wright's journals from 1945 reveal quite clearly his deep interest in the problems of Harlem, especially among its juveniles, and in the Wiltwyck School and its assumptions and methods. On several occasions he discussed his work-in-progress "Rite of Passage" (then called "The Jackal") with a black social psychiatric caseworker at Wiltwyck, who visited Wright at his home and facilitated Wright's visit to the school. In fact, through this caseworker, and usually in his company, Wright visited, over a four-month period, several schools, courts, and other institutions concerned with juvenile delinquency, as he gathered material for his new work. Wright was even drawn willingly into fund-raising efforts for Wiltwyck, and was present on March 6, 1945, when Eleanor Roosevelt, the wife of President Franklin D. Roosevelt, was guest of honor at a tea organized to raise funds for the school. Wiltwyck stood in contrast to the growing hopelessness and cynicism that seemed to plague social work among the black youth of New York, with overburdened caseworkers and overwhelmed judges and little official understanding, apparently, of the special circumstances in the black community. To Wright, Wiltwyck stood as a beacon of enlightenment. "I'm convinced that Wiltwyck is a damn good cause," he confided to his journal, "because it is trying to rehabilitate broken boys, emotionally smashed boys who need a chance."

It should be understood that as much as Wright admired Wiltwyck and the men and women who administered its program on a daily basis, he had few illusions about the motives behind many of its supporters. In his journal, he recorded his reservations about the mentality of those who made the donations on which Wiltwyck increasingly depended. He knew that Wiltwyck could "take care of but a few of the many who need attention." Although he had long since broken with the Communist Party, he believed that "only a revolution" could help the many, as opposed to the few. Why, then, did these donors give large sums of money? "What do they get out of this giving? I cannot but think that there is a delicate element of sadism in it all." These reservations about philanthropy, as opposed to far-reaching social and political changes that would attack head-on the problem of juvenile delinquency, should not be mistaken for cynicism. Wright was being characteristically tough-minded in addressing social problems. To adapt one of his famous remarks about the reception of his collection of stories *Uncle Tom's Children*, he did not wish to join "bankers' daughters" and weep over the misfortunes of the black poor. Rather he wanted everyone to understand the naked truth about juvenile delinquency in Harlem, the causes of the problem, and how precisely it might be solved.

The month after the tea with Mrs. Roosevelt, Wright agreed to write a brochure to help raise money for the school; this led to his draft "Notes for a Booklet," which he later incorporated into "Children of Harlem," intended as a book-length study. In "Notes for a Booklet," Wright gave four examples of boys whose psychological troubles were poorly addressed by the courts and the welfare system, but who might be helped by the intensive, highly scientific work of Wiltwyck in which he believed. Clearly a person identified as "Boy A" became the central character of *Rite of Passage*, Johnny Gibbs. (This is not to say that Wright met the boy at Wiltwyck. However, the boy was definitely of the kind Wiltwyck was designed to help.)

Although slight changes in aspects of this case

137

entered the text from draft to draft, the central elements remained the same. A young black woman goes to a dance, becomes drunk, is seduced, and becomes pregnant. By the time she discovers her condition, she has long lost touch with her child's father. She declines into mental illness about the same time that she gives birth to a normal, healthy boy. She sinks further into *dementia praecox* (now more commonly called schizophrenia). At six months, the boy is given to a foster family. Unaware of his origins, he prospers in almost every way. Then, at six years of age (elsewhere, he is five), the authorities insist on transferring him to a new home and new foster parents. His protests are in vain. He also discovers the truth about his real mother and father, although he is too young to grasp the full significance of what he is told. Rebelling, he begins the downward slide into delinquency.

138

The major difference between this case study and Johnny Gibbs of *Rite of Passage* lies in the age at which the latter is forced to change his foster home. In *Rite of Passage*, Johnny Gibbs is fifteen years old. In the case study, the authorities are faceless and arbitrary, which accurately reflects Wright's sense of the bureaucracy in charge of delinquent children, as opposed to the Wiltwyck approach. Although it is more difficult to believe that even the most arbitrary authorities would remove a child without reason from a home he has known happily for fifteen years, Wright clearly believed that such insensitivity was well within the scope of the New York welfare machine, certainly where African American children and families were concerned. More importantly, he obviously also believed that the switch from six to fifteen years of age gave him far more freedom as an artist seeking to depict the consequences of child neglect and subsequent delinquency.

By making teenaged boys the focus of his story, Wright gave himself the necessary room to develop his commitment as a writer to fiction that involved crime and violence. As I have pointed out, most of his works of fiction involve a crime, a flagrant transgression of the law, frequently accompanied by violent acts against other human beings. Such a crime probably stood for him as a metaphor for human relationships at their most dangerous. To the most despairing and dehumanized people, crime could be, paradoxically, an act of creativity. In *Native Son*, Wright reached the zenith in his employment of crime as a metaphor for human creativity. In killing Mary

139

Dalton and his girlfriend, Bessie, and accepting his authorship of these acts, Bigger takes the first step toward achieving an identity with which he can live. "What I killed for," he declares, "I am." In his inhumane acts Bigger finds the way to the first signs of humanity in his life, as he takes responsibility for his actions.

In *Rite of Passage*, the main episodes of violence involve the bloody, vicious fight between Johnny and Baldy, on the one hand, and the mugging of an innocent man on the other. In contrast to the characters in *Native Son*, no one achieves humanity by acknowledging reponsibility, although each of the gang members, apart from Johnny, seems as brutalized as Bigger. In Johnny's case, however, the fight with Baldy—Johnny's recognition that he must now be tough and hard if he is to survive in his new world—marks his emergence, at least at one level, into manhood. His part in the mugging of an innocent victim brings him face-to-face with certain of the crucial moral dimensions of manhood. The voice of the woman (it is immaterial whether or not she is real) challenges him, and at that moment he challenges himself—by responding to her voice—to justify not simply the act of violence but the entire new life he appears to be starting. (As Wright drafted his story, he was also fascinated by a development he did not employ finally in *Rite of Passage*: the idea to have the boys kidnap a black woman and then hold her captive, out of fear of the consequences to themselves of letting her go. This would allow him to exploit further the psychologies of the various gang members.)

As violent as Wright's fiction often was, and as *Rite of Passage* is in places, he was by no means gratuitously violent or sensational in such episodes. In *Rite of Passage*, his primary concern is the psychology of the delinquent youths. Developing the plot, Wright sought to find "the seeds" for a "good psychological study," as he wrote in his journal. More than by the bloody consequence of rage, he was fascinated by "the whole psychology of anger," which he called "a terribly complex thing [that] ought to be gone into more closely." In judging the merits of a plot that would include the kidnaped black woman, Wright noted: "I have many opportunities here to deal with these boys' emotions,—their relations to their families, their friends, their ultimate hopes." Concerned about understanding the mentality that drove the delinquents to their antisocial acts, Wright probed the possibility of unresolved and conflicted Oedipal fixations; in his

journals, he even pondered the possibility of a relationship between the most common ghetto obscenity
("mother——") in the mouths of young men and
"the incest complex."

Rite of Passage sets out for us many of the principal factors involved in the deterioration of youth culture in the black community of New York City in the
1940s, with an accuracy that still helps us to understand the phenomenon of similar delinquency today.
Although it depicts certain of the juveniles more as
parodies of humanity than as dignified individuals, it
seeks to locate and understand the causes of this loss
of dignity and humanity rather than to rest in censure
of and contempt for the young.

Thus Wright remained faithful in *Rite of Passage*
to the charge he consciously or unconsciously set
himself in building his writing career starting out in
the 1930s: to depict, without fear or compromise, the
truth about the lives of black Americans as he knew
them, without sparing the sensitivities of either the
victims or the perpetrators of the social injustice
fueled by slavery, segregation, and racism in the
United States. He, too, calls out: "YOU BOYS! YOU
BOYS!" He calls out in outrage but also out of a

sense of love and connectedness, or community. And thus he also calls out to the reader, reminding us of our collective responsibility to guard and guide the young, and to be just and fair to all those over whom we have power.

Arnold Rampersad
Princeton University

Selected Bibliography

UNCLE TOM'S CHILDREN, 1938 (stories)

NATIVE SON, 1940 (novel)

TWELVE MILLION BLACK VOICES,
1941 (photo essay)

BLACK BOY, 1945 (autobiography)

THE OUTSIDER, 1953 (novel)

BLACK POWER: *A Report of Reactions
in a Land of Pathos*, 1954 (study)

SAVAGE HOLIDAY, 1954 (novel)

THE COLOR CURTAIN: *A Report on the
Bandung Conference*, 1956

PAGAN SPAIN, 1957 (study)

WHITE MAN, LISTEN!, 1957 (lectures)

THE LONG DREAM, 1958 (novel)

EIGHT MEN, 1961 (stories)

LAWD TODAY!, 1963 (novel)

Chronology

1908 Birth of Richard Nathaniel Wright, first son to Nathan and Ella (born Wilson), on September 4, on a plantation in Roxie, near Natchez, Mississippi.

1912–20 The Wrights move from Natchez to Memphis, Tennessee, then to Elaine, and finally to West Helena, Arkansas. His father having deserted the family, Richard suffers from hunger and poverty, and learns the ways of the streets. In 1915 he and his brother Leon (b. 1910) are placed in an orphanage.

1925 After his mother suffers repeated illnesses, she and the two boys return to her family in Mississippi. Richard receives his diploma from the Smith Robertson High School in Jackson, Mississippi, on June 29. He scrapes together enough money to go to Memphis, Tennessee, and there finds a job and makes his first attempts at serious writing.

1927–32 He leaves Memphis for Chicago in December 1927. Once in Chicago he works at a succession of odd jobs to support himself and later his family. Unable to find a job for a few months because of the Depression, he applies at the Cook County Relief Station for temporary assistance. During this time he continues to explore "great literature" and struggles with his own writing.

1933 Wright joins the Chicago John Reed Club, a literary club, and later the Communist Party, and begins work on two novels and some short stories.

1934 In January two of Wright's poems, "Rest for the Weary" and "A Red Love Note," are published by *Left Front*, and by April he is co-editor of the magazine. *The Anvil* prints his "Strength" and "Child of the Dead and Forgotten Gods," and in June his poem "I Have Seen Black Hands" is accepted by *New Masses*.

1935 Wright is admitted to the Illinois Federal Writers' Project in April and attends the first congress of the League of American Writers in New York as a delegate. The October 8 issue of *New Masses* publishes Wright's first piece of journalism, "Joe Louis Uncovers Dynamite."

1936 From September to November Wright works as a publicity agent for the Chicago Federal Negro Theater and helps Charles DeSheim produce Paul Green's *Hymn to the Rising Sun*, but the play is suppressed. He continues working on the novellas later included in *Uncle Tom's Children*.

148

1937 In June he leaves for New York City, helps launch *New Challenge*, and becomes editor of the Harlem Bureau of the *Daily Worker*.

1938 In February Wright wins the *Story* magazine contest with "Fire and Cloud," and on March 25 his volume *Uncle Tom's Children: Four Novellas* is published by Harper & Brothers.

1938–39 Wright works on *Native Son*. "Fire and Cloud" receives the O. Henry Memorial Prize. In August 1939 he marries Dhimah Meadman.

1940 In January the short story "Almos' a Man" is published in *Harper's Bazaar*. *Native Son* is published in March by Harper & Brothers, is a Book-of-the-Month Club selection, and becomes a best seller. Wright's marriage falters, and ends in divorce. He begins research for *Twelve Million Black Voices*. In October Harper & Brothers publishes *Uncle Tom's Children: Five Long Stories*.

1941 He marries Ellen Poplar on March 12. On March 25 a dramatization of *Native Son*, produced by John Houseman and directed by Orson Welles, opens on Broadway. A daughter, Julia, is born. On November 15 *Twelve Million Black Voices* is published by Viking Press.

1942–43 Following a lecture on growing up in America at Fisk University, Wright starts work on his autobiography. He also completes a first version of "The Man Who Lived Underground."

1944 In August *The Atlantic Monthly* publishes Wright's "I Tried to Be a Communist," which marks the beginning of the Party's open hostility toward him.

1945 A Book-of-the-Month Club selection for February, *Black Boy*, published by Harper & Brothers, becomes an instant best seller. From June to September the Wrights vacation in Canada, and then from October to December he tours the north and west of the U.S. lecturing on African-American literature.

1946 In May the Wrights sail to France as official guests of the French government. In France they live in the Latin Quarter in Paris for several months and make friends with Gertrude Stein.

1947–48 In January 1947 the Wrights return to the U.S., summer on Long Island, and sail back to Paris in August. Wright helps Leopold Senghor, Aimé Césaire, and Alioune Diop launch *Présence Africaine*.

1949 On January 17, 1949, a second daughter, Rachel, is born to the Wrights. In December he sponsors the Gary Davis movement for peace and world citizenship.

1950 At the end of August Wright leaves Europe with film director Pierre Chenal to shoot *Native Son* in Chicago and Buenos Aires. He plays Bigger Thomas in the film.

1951 Back in Paris, Wright founds the Franco-American Fellowship.

1952 Wright spends a few months in London, where he writes the final version of his novel *The Outsider*.

1953 *The Outsider* is published in March and receives some adverse criticism. Wright spends the summer in the Gold Coast (now Ghana) gathering material for a travel diary.

1954 *Black Power: A Report of Reactions in a Land of Pathos* is completed in May. Wright spends August and September touring Spain for another travel narrative. On September 22 *Black Power* is published.

1955 Wright spends a month in Spain, prior to a trip to Indonesia, where he is to report on the Bandung Conference held in mid-April.

1956 Wright is instrumental in organizing the first Congress of Negro Writers and Artists. During the fall he tours Germany and Scandinavia lecturing on Africa, on the psychological problems of oppressed people, and on Afro-American literature.

1957 *Pagan Spain* is published by Harper & Brothers on February 20. In October Doubleday publishes *White Man, Listen!*, a collection of lectures.

1958 *The Long Dream* is published by Doubleday. Wright is refused permission to live in London by British officials.

1959 On May 27 Wright's adaptation of Louis Sapin's *Daddy Goodness* is produced by the USIS company. After visiting Africa, during the summer Wright falls ill from amoebic dysentery and is hospitalized in the American Hospital in Neuilly, France, where he starts writing his haiku.

1960 In March Wright is quite ill from recurring attacks of amoebic dysentery picked up during his travels. In June and in August he records a series of talks on his writings and on the racial situation for French radio. On November 28 around 11 P.M. Wright dies unexpectedly at the Clinique Gibez, where he was spending a week resting and expecting a checkup. He is cremated at the cemetery of Père Lachaise on December 3. The following Wright works were published posthumously: *Eight Men* (1961), *Lawd Today!* (1963), and *American Hunger* (1977).